'It isn't quite as simple as that, is it?' Matthew queried.

'You're not an open, easy-to-read person, are you? You keep yourself to yourself.'

Becky frowned at him. 'I don't know how you've managed to form that opinion,' she said tautly.

'Don't you? For most of the time since I came to this practice, you've been reserved and distant, putting up barriers. . .' His glance narrowed on her. 'But perhaps we made a bad start.'

'Perhaps we did,' she admitted carefully. 'But that doesn't necessarily mean things are likely to change. You have to learn to accept me as I am.'

D1589934

When **Joanna Neil** discovered Mills & Boon, her life-long addiction to reading crystalised into an exciting new career writing medical romances. Her characters are probably the outcome of her varied lifestyle which includes working as a clerk, typist, nurse and infant teacher. She enjoys dressmaking and cooking at her Leicestershire home. Her family includes a husband, son and daughter, an exuberant yellow Labrador and two slightly crazed cockatiels.

Recent titles by the same author:

UNEXPECTED COMPLICATIONS

FAMILY TIES

BY
JOANNA NEIL

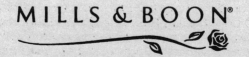

MILLS & BOON®

For Keeley

DID YOU PURCHASE THIS BOOK WITHOUT A COVER?
If you did, you should be aware it is **stolen property** as it was
reported *unsold and destroyed* by a retailer. Neither the Author
nor the publisher has received any payment for this book.

*All the characters in this book have no existence outside the imagina-
tion of the author, and have no relation whatsoever to anyone bearing
the same name or names. They are not even distantly inspired by any
individual known or unknown to the author, and all the incidents are
pure invention.*

*All Rights Reserved including the right of reproduction in whole or
in part in any form. This edition is published by arrangement with
Harlequin Enterprises II B.V. The text of this publication or any part
thereof may not be reproduced or transmitted in any form or by any
means, electronic or mechanical, including photocopying, recording,
storage in an information retrieval system, or otherwise, without the
written permission of the publisher.*

*This book is sold subject to the condition that it shall not, by way of
trade or otherwise, be lent, resold, hired out or otherwise circulated
without the prior consent of the publisher in any form of binding or
cover other than that in which it is published and without a similar
condition including this condition being imposed on the subsequent
purchaser.*

*MILLS & BOON and MILLS & BOON with the Rose Device
are registered trademarks of the publisher.*

*First published in Great Britain 1997
Harlequin Mills & Boon Limited,
Eton House, 18-24 Paradise Road, Richmond, Surrey TW9 1SR*

© Joanna Neil 1997

ISBN 0 263 80078 4

*Set in Times 10 on 11 pt. by
Rowland Phototypesetting Limited
Bury St Edmunds, Suffolk*

03-9704-59323-D

*Printed and bound in Great Britain
by Mackays of Chatham PLC, Chatham*

CHAPTER ONE

BECKY frowned, contemplating the various designs of wallpaper on display and wishing she were somewhere else. She pushed back the tendrils of chestnut hair that had fallen across her cheek, and then eased the wire basket, already filled with rolls of border prints, into a more comfortable position on her arm.

Perhaps it hadn't been such a good idea, after all, to come shopping after work. It had been more than usually hectic at the health centre today, with one of the staff going off sick and everyone else trying to fit in an extra workload, and what she'd really like to do was to kick off her shoes and curl up in a chair by the fire with a good book. Not that there was much chance of that happening for a while yet.

She hadn't reckoned on the shopping taking quite so long, and it was beginning to bother her that Sophie would have been home for a couple of hours now. It shouldn't matter, of course, not under normal circumstances. Her sister would have come home from school like any other teenager and they'd have talked later, each with their own separate plans for the evening. But their lives weren't normal, were they? They hadn't been for some time.

She sighed inwardly. Sophie *was* nearly sixteen, after all, and to all outward appearances she seemed to have accepted the way things were... Was that ever truly possible, though? Was there ever be a time when you could come to accept the loss of both your parents? Her blue eyes closed briefly as she fought the bleak memories.

Perhaps Drew was right. 'You worry too much,' he

was always saying. But how did you *not* worry? She'd been responsible for her sister for too long to be able to take things lightly, and sometimes she felt much older than her twenty four years. There'd been so many changes in their lives, taking a toll on both of them, and all she could do was to be there for Sophie, as the one steadfast, reliable part of her life.

Her glance went to the store's plate-glass windows. It was dark outside. That was one thing she disliked about late autumn—that darkness fell so early. People were hurrying to catch buses, wanting to get home at the end of the day, and she'd dearly have liked to do the same, only there were still a few bits she had to buy before she could do that.

Opening out a roll of paper, she went to study the pattern under a better light, until a movement to one side of her caught her attention, and her glance flickered towards the figure of a woman standing at the far end of the aisle.

She looked to be in her late forties, with black hair that was streaked with grey, and there was something about her that made Becky pause, uncertain for a moment. Was there something vaguely familiar about that face? She didn't look well, though it was hard to pinpoint exactly what might be wrong.

Perhaps it was the way she was standing, leaning slightly forward, her hand resting on the handle of a pushchair as though she needed its support. There wasn't a vestige of colour in her face, and Becky felt all her nursing instincts come rushing to the fore. Ought she to go over and offer help? It could be that she was waiting for someone, minding her grandson while his mother went off to search for something she needed to buy. It was stiflingly crowded in here, and there were so many display tubs overflowing with goods designed to catch the eye that it would have been awkward getting a pushchair around.

Just then, the woman straightened and turned to look at something, and Becky shrugged lightly, relieved that her instincts had proved wrong. Maybe she had simply been bored with waiting.

She glanced down at the paper in her hands, turning back the way she'd come. This pattern was just what she'd been looking for. It was what Sophie had said she liked the other week—

'Oh—' Her elbow made contact with something unyielding, and the impact sent the roll flying from her hands. There was a muffled kind of grunt, and she just had time to see that she had connected with a hard male ribcage, before things became confused.

She stumbled backwards, feeling the hard edge of a wire display unit jabbing the small of her back, and there was a series of thuds as an assortment of the hardware store's sale goods tumbled to the floor. She might have followed them but for a pair of strong hands that grasped her firmly and hauled her upright once more.

'Are you OK?' The voice was deep and warm, stirring her senses in a way that made her heart begin to thump. Winded a little, Becky struggled to gather in a breath and brush away the cloud of dark curls that had tumbled down across her eyes. Blinking rapidly, she found herself focusing on a powerfully masculine physique that left her feeling decidedly shaky. Her legs were suddenly unaccountably weak, and she became aware of a tingling warmth where his fingers had closed on her arms.

'Uh. . .I'm fine. . .I think. . . I'm not exactly sure what happened.'

'You walked into me just as I was coming round the corner,' he said. Still retaining his steadying hold on her, he carefully eased himself away from the rolls of wallpaper that stuck out from the edges of her wire basket and had rammed themselves firmly against his midriff. 'Perhaps you had your mind on other things?'

'I'm sorry,' she said, conscious that she was being

shrewdly assessed by a pair of green eyes that were
unusually flecked with gold. 'There isn't much room to
move in here, is there?' It was an odd feeling, being
surveyed in that curious fashion. It left her feeling
uncomfortably breathless, though that could be put down
to the collision, of course, or maybe it was the fact that
he was still holding her. 'Maybe it wasn't such a good
idea, after all, to come shopping straight after work,
though it seemed logical enough when I thought about
it this morning. It was the sale that did it. I thought I
might pick up a bargain or two.'

She paused momentarily, aware that she was babbling,
and cast a swift glance over his lean, muscled length.
'I'm sorry if I did you any damage,' she added, though
she suspected it would take more than a run-in with a
distracted female to make a dent in him. Beneath the
expensive looking cloth of his grey suit and the clean
lines of his linen shirt, his shoulders were unmistakably
wide, his hard body tapering to a firm, narrow waist and
long, strong legs.

His mouth made a brief, dismissive twist that broke
up the hard-boned angularity of his features and caused
strange things to happen to the rhythm of her pulse. 'You
didn't. Nothing permanent, anyway.'

He seemed to realise then that his hands were still
clasped around her, because he let go of her and bent to
make a start on picking up some of the scattered display.
Becky put down her basket and looked down at his dark
head, absently noting the way the light picked out the
sheen of his black hair. He had nice hair, she thought
irrelevantly, short and crisply styled, so that you could
imagine running your fingers through it.

Lord, what was she thinking? Embarrassed by the turn
her mind had taken, she collected herself and bent down
alongside him, a little flustered, helping him to stack
paint rollers and brushes and put them into some sort of
order on the shelves.

When they had finished, they both straightened, and his glance moved over her, taking in the stone coloured trench coat that hung open, and shifting over her softly rounded figure, her curves gently accentuated by the smooth fit of her dark blue nurse's uniform, before sliding down over the smooth shapeliness of her legs. His gaze lingered a moment, making her skin heat in response, and she drew in a swift, silent breath, annoyed that she should be affected by a mere glance.

'Do you work in town?' he asked. 'At the hospital?'

She shook her head. 'At a health centre. I'm a practice nurse.'

'Really? I expect that's a lot less wearing than having to cope with the routine of a busy hospital. Do you enjoy it?'

She nodded. She'd taken on the role almost a year ago, and though it had turned out to be very different from what she'd been used to at the Royal she was glad she'd made the change. 'Yes, I do, though I wouldn't say it was any less taxing than working in a hospital— at least, these last couple of weeks haven't turned out that way. We're short-staffed and we've been rushed off our feet. One of the doctors has moved on, and the locum isn't due to start until tomorrow, so we're all feeling the extra workload.'

She moved the basket on her arm to ease the weight a little, and he scanned the contents. 'From the looks of things you're going to be just as busy at home.'

She sent him a rueful grin. 'You're right. I moved house a few weeks ago, and I decided I ought to get around to decorating some time, and put my own stamp on the place. Not that I'm looking forward to it. Papering has never been my strong point.'

'But sometimes it just has to be done,' he murmured, smiling faintly. 'Do you live locally?'

A sense of caution stirred in her. She didn't know this man from Adam, but she was beginning to sense that he wouldn't mind getting to know *her*. She hadn't missed that gleam of interest, but that didn't mean she was about to respond to it. Her life was fraught with enough uncertainty at the moment.

She owed him something, however, if only polite conversation, since she'd assaulted him, albeit unintentionally, with fairly lethal weapons, and he'd been good enough not to make a great fuss about it. So she said noncommittally, 'I live a few miles from here. I'm renting a house from one of the doctors who works at the health centre. She married some time ago—the boss, as it happens,' she added with a smile, 'and she moved into her husband's home after the wedding.'

Sarah Lancaster had said she was quite happy for Becky to add her own homely touches to the place, and Becky was hoping that this would be a fresh start for herself and Sophie. Sophie hadn't shown much enthusiasm for the move as yet, but there was time enough for that to change, and they couldn't have gone on the way they were. Their parents' house had been too much to manage, with just the two of them rattling around in those big rooms and the large garden becoming more of a burden as time went on. Besides, Sarah's cottage was nearer to the health centre, as well as being close to Sophie's school.

The man shifted position slightly, and she became aware of people trying to get by. Carefully, she lifted her wire basket out of the way and stepped to one side, trying to avoid the display bins that were blocking the passage.

'I should go,' she said awkwardly, conscious that she was being pushed closer to him as people eased by. She was disturbingly aware of his long-limbed body, the top of her head just about level with his chin. She could feel the expensive cloth of his jacket brushing her arm, his hands moving to help her out of the way—hands that both looked and felt strong and capable, and whose hold on her made her pulse accelerate in a heart-stopping way.

'Must you?' he asked, a darting glimmer in his green eyes. 'I thought we might talk a little more. . .over a drink, perhaps?'

'I don't think that would be a good idea,' she muttered, breaking away from that disturbing contact just as soon as she was able. She hadn't been prepared for the impact that his lean, taut body had had on her oddly heightened senses, and she didn't want to think about why her pulse was beginning to hammer so loudly in her ears. The man was a stranger to her, she couldn't possibly be reacting to him the way she seemed to be.

'Why not?' he persisted, smiling down at her. 'What are you afraid of?'

'I. . .nothing,' she said, shaken to find that for a wild moment she had almost wavered. His dark brow lifted fractionally, and she took in a deep breath. It had been a long day, and now she was beginning to feel the effects of rushing around trying to be in two places at once, that was all. Besides, there was Sophie to think of. With one thing and another, her plans were rapidly coming apart at the seams. 'I don't think I owe you any explanations,' she told him firmly, 'and anyway, I'm very late. Thank you for helping me, but now I really must go.'

She was aware of his gaze narrowing on her, but she hurried away from him before he could delay her any longer. He probably wasn't used to being thwarted in any way, but that was his problem, wasn't it? It was more than time she was home, and she still had to buy wallpaper paste—simple enough, surely? Except that her mind seemed to be refusing to function properly any more. Her concentration had been shot to pieces, and perhaps that wasn't surprising, all things considered.

After a moment's indecision, she tossed a packet of paste into her basket and moved away, checking items off the shopping list in her head with a determined effort.

Within a few moments, she was heading for the check-

out. There she handed over the money for her purchases
and packed the things away in two serviceable navy bags
before starting towards the door. Only, before she
reached it, she recognised the woman she'd seen earlier,
and this time it was clear that something was wrong.

A faint beading of sweat had broken out on the
woman's brow, and she looked as though she was about
to crumple at any moment. Abandoning the bags on the
floor, Becky hurried over to her.

A younger woman was by her side, coping with shopping and pushchair, and trying to move both out of the
way of passers by. She looked worried and harassed at
the same time.

'Is something wrong?' Becky asked. ''Is there anything I can do to help? I'm a nurse.'

'My mother's not feeling well,' the younger woman
said, sounding faintly relieved. 'I need to go and bring
the car around to the front of the store so that I can help
her straight into it and get her home.'

Becky nodded. 'You go and see to it, then. I'll look
after your mother.'

'Would you? If you're sure...? Thanks. I'll be as
quick as I can.'

As she hurried away with the child in the pushchair,
the older woman seemed to slump a fraction, and Becky
put out a supporting arm. 'What's wrong, love? Do you
feel faint?'

'Yes...' The voice wavered. 'And sick...I feel
sick...I think I need to sit down for a while.'

'I'm sure we can find somewhere,' Becky said, signalling discreetly with her eyes to one of the assistants who
had seen what was happening. Between them they helped
the ashen faced woman to a bench by the window.

'We don't have anywhere more private,' the girl apolo-
gised. 'Will this do?'

'I think we'll manage,' Becky answered briefly. 'I

wonder if you could fetch a glass of water? And perhaps a cool cloth might help.'

'I'll go and see to it.' The girl vanished and Becky gave her attention to the woman once more.

'Just lie quite still for a while,' she murmured, 'and I'll put something under your feet to raise them a little.' She took off her coat, rolling it up and placing it carefully on the bench underneath the woman's legs. 'Has this happened to you before?'

'No. At least, not in public,' the woman added weakly. 'I feel such a fool.'

'Don't you worry about that,' Becky said firmly. 'It can happen to anyone. Are you wearing anything tight?'

The woman shook her head, and when the assistant returned a few moments later Becky dipped the cloth she brought into the cold water and wrung it out, gently wiping the woman's face, until, after a few minutes she began to look as though she might be recovering a little.

'Have you any idea what could have brought this on?' Becky asked quietly. 'Have you missed out on a meal, perhaps?'

'No, I haven't. It's the pain in my back, I think. I felt it coming on earlier, building up. It seemed to happen so quickly. It's such a nuisance, I feel so silly.'

Becky looked at her thoughtfully. 'Is it a pain you've had before? Are you on any kind of medication for it?'

'It just bothers me from time to time, and then I take painkillers. I took some a few minutes ago.'

'And is it easing off at all?'

'Yes...yes, I feel much better now,' the woman added, struggling to sit up. 'It's very kind of you to stop and help like this.'

'You just lie still for a bit longer,' Becky murmured, giving her a smile and exerting gentle pressure on her shoulder. 'I'm glad that I was here and able to do something. Have you been to see your doctor about the pain in your back?'

'Not recently. I went to see her about a year ago. I'm
not sure Dr Lancaster's still at the health centre, though.
I heard she had a baby some months ago.'

'Ah!' Light dawned at last for Becky. 'I thought I
knew your face from somewhere. You're a patient at the
Soar Bridge Centre, aren't you? That's where I work.'

'I wondered about that. . .I wasn't sure. I'm
Helen Mason.'

Becky smiled, glad that the small puzzle had been
solved. 'Obviously you're not a regular visitor there,
Helen, but I think if the pain is bad enough to make you
feel faint it might be a good idea for you to make an
appointment and have a check-up. You're right about Dr
Lancaster. She works part-time now, but if you don't get
to see her you could always see her husband. It could
simply be that you need to strengthen the muscles
that support the spine. There are exercises you can do
that might help—unless, of course, you're already
doing some?'

Helen Mason shook her head. 'I suppose I ought to
see someone. Perhaps I'll phone the surgery.'

She was silent for a while, resting, and after a few
minutes Becky said quietly, 'Here comes your daughter.
Perhaps you'd like some water to drink?' She helped her
to sit up. 'Take your time, there's no rush.'

The younger woman hurried towards them. 'I've got
the car just out front, Mum,' she said. 'How are you
feeling? Are you well enough to move?'

'Yes, I'm fine; I'll be all right.' Mrs Mason still looked
shaky but she had a little more colour now in her face.
She took a few more sips of water, then handed the glass
back to Becky.

'Thanks,' she said. 'You've been very kind.'

'Can you manage?'

'Yes, thank you, we'll be fine now.'

Becky watched them go, then looked at her watch
and hurried over to the checkout where she had left her

shopping. The man whom she'd seen earlier was talking
to the assistant who'd helped her, and for a second or
two her equilibrium deserted her. She felt his gaze swing
in her direction as she picked up the bags.

'Wait,' he said, frowning, but Becky pulled herself
together and shook her head.

'I can't,' she muttered, moving swiftly towards the
exit. 'Sorry.' She was determined that she wasn't going
to be delayed any longer. She had to go; she had to get
home. There was the evening meal to prepare; it was
important that Sophie ate at regular intervals, being diabetic. Not that she ought to need reminding, but Sophie
was at a difficult age, and sometimes she didn't seem to
take her illness as seriously as she should.

He called to her again as she hurried outside the store
into the darkness, where the streetlamps spilled pools of
light over the pavement, and she heard muffled sounds,
a slight skirmishing, as though he was coming after her
but people were getting in his way.

He wasn't following her, was he? Didn't the man know
when he was getting the brush-off? She hardly dared
risk a look around, but she had to be sure. Yes, he'd left
the shop, and he was heading her way, his gaze locking
with hers until his path was blocked by a woman with a
baby in one arm and a buggy she was trying unsuccess-
fully to fold with the other. He stopped long enough to
help her, and Becky took her chance and sped away
from him. Even so, she heard him cut short the woman's
grateful thanks, and she didn't miss his muttered
expletive which he must have uttered as he saw her
making her getaway.

He was certainly persistent, this man, and it made her
even more convinced that she ought to lose him. He'd
seemed decent enough, but how could you tell for sure?
He wasn't taking no for an answer and that was worrying.
Thank heaven she wasn't too far from the car park. Seeing the building loom in the distance, she put on a spurt,

sending up a silent prayer that he wouldn't catch up with her.

At last she reached the entrance and hurried through it towards the lift, whose doors were miraculously open, waiting. She rushed into it, breathing fast now as she hit the button for her floor. She could hear his footsteps coming after her. Her heart was beginning to thump heavily as fear stole through her veins and knotted her stomach, and she closed her eyes in a brief moment of thankfulness as the doors closed quickly on her. She hadn't seen him take the stairs but she hoped she'd make it to her level, and the car, before he could find her again.

Fate must have been with her, because she didn't see any sign of him as she hurtled into the driving seat and started the ignition. Perhaps she'd managed to give him the slip after all.

It was odd that he'd tried to follow her, that he'd gone to such lengths to try to talk to her again in the face of her resistance. It just went to show that you couldn't be too careful. She turned the car onto the dark main road and headed away from town. Traffic was fairly heavy and she couldn't tell whether she had lost him completely, but she thought she probably had. Maybe she ought to think about getting a personal alarm.

Relief came slowly, her pulse slowing to a more natural rhythm as she approached the street where she lived. There were lights on in the house when she drew the car to a halt at the kerbside, and the sight gladdened her as she pushed her key into the lock of the front door.

'You're late,' Sophie said as she walked into the hall. There was a faint note of accusation in her voice, and she looked pale, her features pinched. 'I thought you'd be home over an hour ago.'

'I'm sorry, love,' Becky said ruefully, dropping her bags and going to give her a hug. She felt Sophie's shoulders sag a little as some of the tension left her. 'A few things happened to delay me, or I'd have been home

much sooner.' That seemed like something of an under-
statement now. 'A woman fainted in the store and I
stayed to help. Were you worried?'

'Just a bit. I thought you might have had an accident.'
Sophie drew herself up straight with an effort that caused
Becky to bite her lip with a twinge of remembered
anguish.

'Nothing like that,' she said quietly. It would take time
for her sister to feel secure again. All she could do was
to provide a solid base for her, to let her know that if it
was humanly possible she would always be here for her.

Sophie pushed back a long strand of brown hair that
had escaped from one of the combs at her temples. 'I'm
making a cup of tea. Do you want one?'

It would take a long while before either of them could
forget the trauma of the night their father hadn't come
home, and Becky wished she hadn't been the cause of
such a painful reminder. But she said simply, 'Tea sounds
wonderful right now. I'd love one. I'll get started on the
meal in a minute, just as soon as I've hung up my coat.'

'No rush. I'm not all that hungry.' At Becky's swift
glance she added defensively, 'I'm not trying to lose any
more weight. I told you—I only wanted to be able to
get into my new skirt for the disco on Saturday.'

'I shouldn't think you'll have a problem with that.'
Becky went to hang up her coat, then carried her bags
through to the kitchen.

'How did it go at school today?' she asked, and Sophie
shrugged.

'OK, I guess. I was thinking about getting a Saturday
job; a lot of the girls are doing that.'

Becky frowned. 'Is that wise with all the school-work
you have to do? You know you'll get more and more
homework as time goes on. This time next year you'll
be working towards A levels.'

'I'm not so sure I want to stay on for that.'

'Mum and Dad would have wanted you to stay on to

get some qualifications,' Becky reminded her, but Sophie pulled a face.

'Would they? How would I know what they'd have felt? Anyway, they aren't around to care, are they? We lost Mum when I was nine, and it's been two years since Dad died. You can't expect me to spend my whole life thinking about what they would have wanted.' Her chin jutted in the defensive way that Becky was coming to recognise.

'They loved you,' she murmured. 'You know that. They always wanted the best for you, for both of us, and it's your future we're talking about, your life.'

'You worry too much,' Sophie retorted dismissively. 'You're not my mother, or my father. You'll be old before your time if you keep telling me what I need to do.'

Sophie was only echoing what Drew had said, and Becky experienced a momentary feeling of self-doubt. Was she wrong? Firmly, she pushed the question to the back of her mind. She could only do what she thought best. She was all Sophie had now, and common sense told her that her sister would argue whatever she said, since she was going through that awful teenage phase of questioning everything.

'We'll talk about it some other time,' she said, accepting the mug of tea that Sophie pushed across the table towards her.

'I'm going to do my homework upstairs,' Sophie announced.

'OK. I'll give you a shout when dinner's ready.' She'd left a chicken to cook in the oven, setting the automatic timer, and as she checked on it now a rich smell of meat and herbs filled the kitchen. Another half-hour should do it. Closing the oven door, she looked back towards the table where she'd left her shopping, but before she could begin to deal with it the doorbell rang.

She frowned, going out into the hall and opening the

front door as far as the safety chain would allow. The man she'd met in the hardware store was standing in the porch, and at the sight of him she froze in shock.

'I almost lost you,' he said grimly. 'Dammit, you were driving as though the devil was at your heels, and if I hadn't taken a guess on the direction you were headed in I might never have caught up.' Becky stared at the hard line of his mouth.

'What on earth are you doing here?' she bit out, her voice rising a notch as she took in the enormity of the fact that he'd followed her all the way from town. Then a surge of annoyance took over. 'You had the gall to come after me,' she snapped. 'Whatever possessed you? Are you mad?'

A muscle flicked in his hard jaw. 'I had no choice; you took off in such a hurry.'

'Look,' Becky said tautly, 'I don't know you, and I don't want to talk to you. I thought I'd made that clear.' She didn't raise her voice any more in case Sophie heard and came down the stairs wondering what was happening. It wouldn't do to let this maniac know that there were just she and her sister in the house. 'Go away and stop pestering me,' she hissed.

'I have to—'

He still wasn't giving up. It was too much, she'd had enough of him, and her temper was rising like quicksilver. Giving the door a hefty shove, she was alarmed to see his fingers come up at the same time to grasp the jamb, and in the next moment the wood of the door slammed against the back of his hand, trapping it there. His harsh shout of pain made her wince, and for a second or two her hold on the door weakened as she stared in breathless horror at the resulting injury. It was clear from the livid weals already rising on his skin that she'd done him some damage.

Clenching his teeth, he withdrew his hand, and she hesitated for only a few seconds longer before instinct took over. She couldn't afford to show him any sympathy. They were two vulnerable girls here, and she wasn't going to let him get so much as a finger through that opening again.

'Go away,' she said again, grimly, 'or I'll call the police.' Then she slammed the door properly shut and pushed home the bolt.

The incident upset her, left her feeling more than a little shaky. She hadn't meant to harm him but he shouldn't have put his hand there. It was his own fault if he'd been hurt.

Glancing up the stairs, she was glad that Sophie had heard nothing. She must be listening to her personal stereo as usual, and for once she was glad that Sophie spent so much time in her own room.

Pulling in a deep breath to steady herself, she went back into the kitchen and set about unloading her bags. He'd surely have gone now—he'd have more sense than to hang around where he wasn't wanted, wouldn't he?

The wallpaper filled one bag, and she took that out and stacked it into a cupboard, going back then to unzip the other and search for the packets of paste she'd bought.

Only, they weren't there. She opened the bag up properly and peered inside, staring at the contents in growing dismay.

'Oh, no,' she whispered as comprehension dawned. 'Oh, no. . .what have I done?' This wasn't her shopping, she didn't recognise any of these things and yet the bag looked like hers—it was the same colour, the same size.

None of her shopping was here. Instead, she saw a couple of large ring-binders crammed full of papers, documents of some sort, along with a few bits and pieces that looked as though they'd come from the store.

Oh, Lord, what had she done? She'd assumed that the man was following her. She'd assumed that he wanted to get to know her, when all the time. . .

Chewing at her lip, she walked slowly back to the front

door and cautiously opened it. His car—she assumed it was his car—was parked in front of the house and he was leaning against it, nursing his injured hand.

Tentatively, she called out to him. 'I think. . .I think there may have been a misunderstanding.'

'Do you?' he gritted. 'I wonder how that can have come about?' His tone was full of dry sarcasm, and she winced before glancing down into the shelter of the porch and saw what must be her own bag deposited neatly on the tiles. She didn't have to look inside to know what she would find.

'Is this my wallpaper paste?' she asked on a humble note.

'That's what it looks like to me,' he tossed back coldly, 'but you'd better check. I shouldn't like you to think I was trying another ploy simply to get to know you.' His frost-laden manner chilled her to the core, leaving her feeling more guilty than ever. His mouth was set in a grim line, and she didn't think it was entirely because of the pain she'd inflicted.

'I'm really sorry,' she told him. 'I didn't know—'

'Just check the contents,' he cut in with knife-like precision. 'Let's not have any more misunderstandings.'

Awkwardly, she did as she was told. 'Paste,' she confirmed. 'Look, I feel very bad about this. Will you come in and let me have a look at your hand? I must have done some damage. . . Is it very bad?'

'Mangled is probably the word I'd use,' he muttered tersely, 'but don't trouble yourself about it. Just swap the bags and I'll go. There are some important papers in my holdall. I need them, otherwise I shouldn't have gone to the trouble of following you.'

'Of course you can have them, but I wish you'd come in,' she repeated. 'I could at least bathe your hand for you. It might stop some of the bruising.'

'I shouldn't want you to think I was a murderer on

the prowl,' he said. 'I think you'd feel much safer if I stayed out here.'

Becky swallowed hard. 'Please let me do what I can to make amends,' she said. 'Anyway, I'm not alone in the house,' she told him. 'I live with someone, and I don't think you'd get far if you did try anything.'

His mouth moved at that, making a kind of derisive twist, but at least he started walking up the path towards her. 'I get the feeling you're perfectly capable of looking after yourself.'

She didn't answer that one, but led him into the house and through to the kitchen. 'Sit down,' she told him. 'I'll just get the first-aid box.' Coming back to him a moment later, she pressed her lips together as she looked at his hand. The skin had been broken, and it was bleeding freely. 'It needs to be cleaned,' she said.

He wasn't arguing with her. 'It looks messier than it is,' he said briefly. 'If you could just cover it up so that I don't bleed over the car upholstery, I'll be on my way.'

'Of course.' He was silent as she worked on the injury, and as she put a dressing in place she murmured diffidently, 'At the checkout, when you called me, you were really just trying to tell me about my mistake, weren't you? I thought—'

'You thought I wanted to chat you up,' he cut in. 'You flatter yourself.'

She deserved that, but it stung all the same. 'I think your hand will do now,' she said. 'It will hurt for a while, I expect, but I don't think anything's broken. Will you be able to drive?'

'I shall manage.' He glanced at her handiwork. 'A neat job. At least your nursing skills can't be faulted.'

She almost flinched at the sarcasm, but offered stoically, 'Can I get you a coffee or anything?' He shook his head, getting to his feet, and she followed him to the door. 'I'm really sorry,' she said again.

His mouth moved in a parody of a smile, and there

was a diamond glitter in his dark eyes as he said coolly, 'Goodnight. I won't say goodbye because I expect I shall see you around.' Then he started down the path to his car.

His words took her aback. There was something in the tone he'd used that made Becky's steps falter. Somehow, it hadn't sounded like a casual dismissal, and her heart squeezed in a peculiar way as she watched him go. It wasn't likely that they would meet again, was it? But that thought did nothing to ease her uncertainty. She'd picked up on something in what he'd said, an odd note, somewhere between a threat or a promise, and she wasn't at all sure she was comfortable with either.

CHAPTER TWO

Sun glinted off the red-roofed buildings of the Soar
Bridge Health Centre as Becky drove into the car park
the next morning. She had been drawn to this place from
the moment she had first set eyes on it, and now she
viewed the scene once more with satisfaction. Mature
trees edged the mellow brick walls, their leaves having
changed colour over the past weeks, orange through red
and gold, and as Becky walked up to the main door her
feet scuffed the damp litter of those that had fallen.

She was early, but Martyn Lancaster, the head of the
centre, was already in Reception. He wasn't alone but
appeared to be deep in conversation with a man who had
his back towards her, and she wondered if this was the
new locum doctor. Something about the long-limbed,
broad-shouldered figure made her pause for a moment,
a vague feeling of recognition assailing her, but then, as
Martyn greeted her, she shrugged off the sensation.

'Becky,' Martyn said, 'let me introduce you to our
new colleague. This is Dr Kingston. Matthew. He'll be
with us for the next few months, up until the new year.'

As the new man turned to face her, Becky's heart
made an odd, painful contraction, the welcoming smile
fading from her lips, and she felt an uncomfortable sinking sensation in the region of her stomach, because Dr
Kingston was not at all what she had expected. He was
no craggy, middle-aged stranger. Instead, his tall, lean
frame was all too disturbingly familiar, those compelling,
carved features ones that she had seen only very recently.
His gaze locked with hers, and she felt her colour rise
in a swift, sweeping tide along her cheekbones.

'Becky is our practice nurse,' Martyn was saying,

oblivious to the suddenly charged atmosphere. 'She's been with us for almost a year, and I'm sure you'll find that she's a great girl to work with. She's very good with the patients and we feel we're lucky to have her.'

'We've already met,' Dr Kingston said abruptly. Green eyes appraised her coolly.

Martyn's surprise showed. 'You have?'

'Quite recently.' He gestured with his injured hand, and Becky felt her heart judder violently. Lord, he wasn't going to relate the whole sorry story, was he? His mouth twisted as though he had read her thoughts. 'I met with an accident,' he went on, 'and she was on the scene and able to deal with it.'

Martyn inspected the wound, now uncovered. 'Nasty,' he murmured. 'How did you come to do that?' he asked.

'I caught it in a door.' His glittering gaze made her pulse accelerate. 'But it's a long story. Remind me to tell you some time.' He used a droll tone, and Becky could feel her temperature rising, the breath snagging in her throat.

Was she really going to have to work with this man? How long would it be before her folly was revealed to the rest of her colleagues and she became the focal point of their dry wit? Dr Kingston probably suspected she was accident-prone, but what other opinions had he formed of her?

In the space of just an hour or so she'd managed to assault him several times, as well as jump to completely the wrong conclusion and make an absolute fool of herself. It was clear from the measured way he looked at her that he wasn't going to take her seriously. She would never be able to convince him that she was a perfectly level headed individual.

'You'll meet the rest of the team later,' Martyn was saying. 'We've been short-handed for a while, since my wife, Sarah, left to have the baby. She only works part-time now that she has Charlotte to look after, and then of course we lost James Castlemaine when he decided to work abroad for a while. We're glad to have you here, Matthew. Believe me, you haven't come a day too soon.'

Becky wasn't so sure that she would echo those sentiments. She'd much rather that anyone but Matthew Kingston had come to take over from James. He was altogether too much, too overwhelmingly...male.

She helped herself to a coffee, hoping it would calm her a little, while Martyn showed Matthew various aspects of Reception. It was much less wearing on her nerves to study him from a distance. Close to, she was far too aware of him.

He was wearing a dark suit today, the jacket sitting well on those wide shoulders, the trousers moulding themselves to his long, muscled legs. He looked incredibly fit, and though at the moment his manner was relaxed and easygoing she knew only too well that appearances could be deceptive. His reactions were quick, definite, and she was pretty certain that his mind was every bit as sharp as the rest of him.

She decided to take her coffee through to her own room, where she held her clinics, but as she started towards the door Martyn delayed her, cutting off her escape.

'You'll be working fairly closely with Matthew,' he told her. 'He's going to be taking the diabetes clinic one afternoon a week, and I think you're the one who is best suited to help him with that. Anyway, I'll leave you two to get further acquainted; I must go and organise my surgery.' To Matthew he added, 'If there's anything you need, just shout.'

'Will do,' Matthew said as Martyn left the room. He sent Becky a cool, measured glance, and for some reason she recalled his ominous words from the night before. 'I expect I shall see you around.'

She expelled a harsh breath, and said accusingly, 'You knew, didn't you, that we'd meet again?'

His attractive mouth made a wry shape. 'I thought it was quite likely. I'd almost guessed as much, from what you were saying in the store, but your home address more or less clinched it.'

Her blue eyes glittered angrily. 'I had no idea who you were, or that you were going to turn up here today. You might have said something about it last night.'

'Might I? I thought you said more than enough for both of us.' He was deliberately trying to rattle her, and her lips tightened.

'Even so—'

'Let's not rake over old coals,' he cut in smoothly, taking the wind right out of her sails. 'We're going to have to work together; that's been established for us, and we might as well get used to the idea. Martyn said that that you were best suited to help with the clinic. Does that mean you're specially trained for working with diabetics?'

She nodded stiffly. 'My sister has diabetes. It was diagnosed about four years ago when I was training and so naturally I took a special interest in the condition. Sophie needs insulin injections daily. I've seen her having to cope with a lot of problems.'

Matthew nodded briefly. 'Then we should talk more about this later—time's getting on, and right now I have to go and check my own surgery list.' It wasn't quite a dismissal—of course he had work to do. So did she; only, that was the very last thing on her mind after he'd succeeded in throwing her completely off balance.

She saw little of him through the rest of the morning, and she was glad about that, because it gave her time to adjust to the shock of coming face to face with him again after last night. The morning passed quickly with a constant flow of patients through the health centre, and most of her time was taken up with doing blood tests and minor dressings, so that she hardly had a moment to herself to update her notes on to the computer. Then

at lunchtime there were several errands that had to be
seen to—a trip to the post office, and another to the
florist to order flowers for Gran's birthday.

In the afternoon, she worked her way steadily through
her list of patients coming in for flu vaccinations.
Matthew Kingston, she learned from a quick check of
the rota, was taking surgery this afternoon. The doctors
worked on an appointments system, and his list was full
to overflowing. Martyn would be spending the afternoon
at the hospital, where he saw patients at the orthopaedic
clinic, and Nick Tyler, the other partner, was out on call.

There were a number of people waiting to see Becky
when one of the receptionists came hurrying through to
her room.

'There's a Mrs Jarrom in Reception,' the girl began.
'She's in a bit of a state about her little boy—he's outside, in the car with his grandmother, at the moment.
She doesn't have an appointment to see the doctor but
she's quite agitated. The child has a high temperature,
she says, and doesn't seem at all well. She wants someone
to see him, but you know how busy we are.

'Do you think you could have a look at him, Becky?
I don't like to disturb Dr Kingston when he already has
so many people to see this afternoon. It might just be a
case of a heavy cold or something—some mothers do
worry unnecessarily.'

'OK,' Becky agreed. 'Send them through.'

Mrs Jarrom was a young woman, slim, bordering on
thin, with short, fly-away brown hair, and she was looking particularly anxious when Becky saw her. In her arms
she held a small boy not much above two years old.

'What seems to be the problem?' asked Becky.

'He's been fretful all day,' the mother began. 'I thought
perhaps he was coming down with something but there
was nothing specific, not enough for me to warrant calling the doctor out. Then he seemed to get worse in the
last hour or so. He's very hot and he won't eat, and that

isn't like him at all; he loves his food usually.'

'Yes, he does look overheated,' Becky murmured, frowning a little as she looked at their small patient. The little boy was obviously unhappy. He was grizzling and rubbing at his eyes, clinging to his mother. 'Has he been vomiting at all?'

Mrs Jarrom nodded. 'Just once, before we got in the car. He says his head hurts, and his neck, and his eyes seem to be troubling him. I'm really worried about him, I think he ought to see one of the doctors. I didn't want to leave it until the doctor on call is available, that might take too long.'

'He doesn't look well, poor little chap,' Becky said thoughtfully. 'Would you mind waiting a moment while I go and have a word with the doctor?'

Becky waited until she saw a patient leaving Matthew's room before knocking on his door.

'Something wrong?' he asked as she entered the room. He looked cool and in control, and his desk was neat, everything in its place as though he disliked clutter. He was obviously a very organised kind of man, and Becky couldn't help wondering how he would react to being interrupted. She'd already made a bad enough start with him.

She pushed her misgivings to one side, though, and told him, 'There's a little boy in my room who doesn't look at all well. I wondered if you'd mind taking a look at him? He has a very high temperature from the looks of things.'

Matthew frowned, and she would have gone on to say more, only he cut in with, 'If you think he needs to see me, you'd better bring him through.'

She went to fetch him. The little boy was clinging to his mother, who was visibly upset, and it took all of Becky's skill and understanding of children to help her persuade the child that the doctor was only going to look at him and try to make him better.

'I think it might be a good idea if you stayed,' Matthew murmured, before turning to smile at the boy. 'Hello, Davey. Would you like to sit on my big couch? You'll be as high as we are then, won't you? Perhaps Mummy can lift you up. . .'

Becky took one or two soft toys over there, and Davey was distracted by them enough to allow Matthew to examine him gently. He was sincere and soothing, and in a moment or two the little boy's grizzles came to a reluctant stop as Matthew gently coaxed him, winning the child's trust with quiet good humour. 'Is your neck hurting? Can you show me where? Just there. . .?' He was thorough, but infinitely tender, and Becky felt a lump come into her throat as she watched him. 'Well done,' he said, when he'd finished. 'What a good lad you are.

'I think you were right to bring him to us,' he said quietly to the mother, while Becky helped her to a seat and settled Davey on her lap. 'He does appear to be quite ill with some kind of infection, and, bearing in mind the various symptoms and how suddenly this has developed, I think he needs to have urgent antibiotic treatment. We should keep a really close eye on him, and I think the best place to do that would be in hospital, where we can find out exactly what it is that we're dealing with.'

Mrs Jarrom had sucked in a shocked breath, but, probably mindful of the child's reaction, she didn't voice her fears but just stared at Matthew in desperate appeal.

'What I want to do, Mrs Jarrom,' Matthew went on, 'is to give him an injection right away and then we'll get on to the hospital and tell them to expect him.'

Mrs Jarrom nodded and hugged the boy to her. 'This injection,' she said, 'will it stop anything from developing, will it make him better?'

'I'm sure that it will help a good deal,' Matthew said. 'The hospital will do tests, of course, to find out exactly what we're dealing with but I must say there's a strong possibility of meningitis. You did well to bring him in so quickly.' He stood up and spoke to Becky then, running briefly through a list of instructions before turning back to the child.

'Davey, I need to give you a little injection. It might sting just a tiny bit, but it'll be over faster than a jet plane, you'll see.'

Becky brought the trolley and syringe to the side of the couch.

'A jet plane?' Davey's eyes widened as Matthew nodded.

'Like that one up there.' As he swabbed the site, he pointed to a collection of model planes and helicopters suspended from the ceiling, then said, 'Here goes... whoosh... and it's all finished. You hardly noticed, did you, looking at all my aeroplanes? I'll see if there's one in my box for you to play with.' Smiling, he retrieved a toy from a brightly coloured box in a corner of the room, while Becky cleared away.

He was a natural with children, she reflected, finishing the task and going to phone the hospital. It had made her feel warm inside, just watching him. Her call was answered in the next moment or two, and she spoke quietly to the duty sister for a while, before signalling to Matthew that they would expect the boy shortly.

'I thought the Hib vaccine was supposed to protect against meningitis?' the mother said, easing the child into a more comfortable position in her arms.

'The problem is,' Matthew explained, 'there are several types of meningococcal infection, but the Hib vaccine only protects against one of them. Try not to worry, though. He'll be in good hands in hospital, and they'll help you to make arrangements to stay with him, if you'd like.'

'What about transport?' Becky asked. 'Shall I arrange for an ambulance?'

'I've got the car outside,' Mrs Jarrom said. 'My mother will drive us. It'll be quicker that way.'

Matthew nodded. 'If that's what you'd rather do, Becky can let them know.'

'Thank you.' She went out a few minutes later and Becky went with her to the car, helping to put the little boy securely into his car seat.

'Would you like someone from the centre to go with you?' Becky asked, but Mrs Jarrom shook her head.

'No, I'll be fine; I know where to go.'

Becky nodded and watched as they drove away from the centre. She'd ring and then check again with the hospital in half an hour or so to see that they had arrived safely. She was glad Matthew had acted promptly, that he hadn't put any barriers in the way of his seeing the child.

Apologising to the patients she'd left waiting, she went on with the vaccination programme until she'd dealt with all her appointments. Around the middle of the afternoon she found time to make her way to the staffroom to grab a quick cup of tea and discovered that Matthew was already in there. She'd expected to find the room empty, and seeing him standing by the window, looking out at the autumn landscape, caused her heart to miss a beat. He turned and looked at her directly, missing nothing of her startled reaction, and she was flustered for a moment.

She sucked in a calming breath. 'How is it going?' she asked him. 'You've had a busy first day.'

'I expect I shall get used to it.'

'I dare say,' Becky returned. 'I'm glad you managed to fit the child in this afternoon. It would have been worrying if he'd had to wait until someone went out to him, perhaps this evening. You were very good with him.'

'So were you,' he said, and she felt her cheeks lightly flush at the compliment. 'It's the worst part of the job, for me,' he went on, 'seeing children distressed and in pain.'

She nodded. 'Me too. I hope he'll be all right. I suppose we might need to find out about contacts with other children.'

'It depends what the verdict is from the hospital, but we'll know that soon enough. According to the mother, he's not been to a playgroup, but if it is meningitis then family members will have to be seen.'

Becky poured milk into her tea and stirred it slowly, before sipping the hot liquid. 'Martyn said you were here until the new year. What happens then? Do you have another job to go to?'

'I'm taking up a partnership in a practice similar to this one, down south.' He moved his shoulders experimentally as though easing a knot of tension there, and a ripple of unfamiliar sensation darted through her as she watched, fascinated by the smooth interplay of muscle and sinew. 'I'm looking forward to it,' he added. 'I seem to have been on the move for the last few years, so it will be good to settle somewhere. I worked in London for a time, then in a country practice, and when this chance of a partnership came along it seemed too good an opportunity to turn down.'

'Do you think you'll like living around here in the meantime? Are you familiar with the area at all?' She put her cup down on a ledge.

'My family live hereabouts—have done for years. I suppose it will mean doing a lot of commuting once I get established in the new place.' He moved over to a table in the middle of the room, where plates had been laid out, temptingly laden with an array of sticky buns. 'These look good,' he murmured. 'Are they here for a special reason? Is it an occasion of some sort?'

She went to join him there, and his hand brushed her arm as she came to his side, sending a shockwave of electricity right through to her fingertips as though she'd connected with a live circuit. She was stunned by the sensation, unable to move for a few seconds, until she made a determined effort to take hold of herself. What was the matter with her? Had her senses gone haywire?

'It's Maria's birthday,' she managed. 'She's one of

the health visitors. It's a tradition here, when someone
has a birthday, to bring in cakes or buns or some such.
Help yourself.'

'I think I will,' he said, smiling, and she was startled
by the change in his features. His looks had been something to write home about before, but now. . . She felt
her toes curl in response. No one should be that good
looking. 'I'm famished if the truth be known,' he added,
interrupting the wild train of her thoughts. 'I didn't have
time for more than a quick snack at lunchtime. Do you
want one?'

She studied the tempting assortment, her hand waver-
ing over the line of her stomach before smoothing over
the curve of her hip. 'Better not,' she murmured.

Matthew raised a brow. 'You're not dieting, are you?'

She felt her face heat. 'Not exactly,' she said, conscious of the arguments she'd had with Sophie on the
subject. Her situation was different, she reasoned, she
had a constant battle to keep herself trim whereas Sophie
had hardly any need to worry about her figure. 'I have
to be careful what I eat,' she said with a grimace, 'otherwise I pile the pounds on.'

'Nonsense,' he said. 'Too many women think they
have to be as thin as rails. Lord knows why.' He studied
her in a way that made her temperature go sky-high, his
glance tracing the full curve of her breasts and coming
to rest on the rounded line of her hips. 'I don't see
anything wrong with your figure.' His green eyes took
on a devilish glitter. 'Quite the opposite, in fact. Anyway,
you'd do far better to walk or take some other kind of
exercise, rather than cut down on food.'

Becky made a face. 'What makes you think I don't?
I like walking and I certainly get plenty of exercise in
this job and at home.'

'There you are, then,' he said with a grin. 'But there
are some good walks round here. Have you tried any of
them lately?'

She shook her head. 'Not recently; there never seems to be enough time.'

'That's a shame,' he said, biting into his bun. 'You said that you'd not long ago moved house. Did you come from far away?'

'Not really. I've lived round here most of my life. My grandfather used to work as a solicitor in the town and my grandmother kept a craft shop until a few years back. I decided to move house so that we could be nearer to the surgery, and things are certainly a lot easier now that I don't have so far to travel. I think I'm going to be a lot happier now, more settled.'

'Perhaps you'll be able to find time to explore the area a little more,' Matthew suggested, licking sugar off his thumb. She watched him, enthralled. How could such a simple gesture be so tantalisingly sensual? she wondered despairingly. Thank heaven he hadn't noticed her absorption. 'Try some of the organised walks, maybe,' he added. 'I joined a local rambling club when I knew I was going to be based here for a while. I used to be a member a few years ago, and they seemed happy to have me join them again.'

It was clear now how he managed to keep himself so fit and athletic-looking—he was a man used to the outdoors.

His skin had a healthy glow, and there was an energy about him, a vitality that spoke of a man who liked to keep on the move.

Perhaps she'd been staring, because his green eyes glinted, and he said casually, 'Why don't you come along?' He was looking at her questioningly, but she made herself stop and think before she answered him. There could be problems in mixing with him outside work. She didn't know him very well, yet, but she sensed that she could very well end up with her fingers burned. Already her reactions to him were enough to confuse and dismay her. It would be much safer to concentrate on building up a professional relationship with him.

'I don't get a lot of free weekends,' she said. 'Not with the move and the decorating and so on. Perhaps later, when I'm more settled, I'll think about it.' She was making excuses and from the sardonic twist of his mouth she wondered if he'd guessed her misgivings.

'I'll keep you to that,' he murmured, his glance darkly mocking.

His determination unnerved her. Conscious that he was continuing to watch her, she finished her tea quickly and pushed it to one side. 'I must get back to work. I have to get ready for my next clinic.'

'Me too,' he said. 'I have patients waiting.'

She was kept busy for the next half hour or so doing blood-pressure and weight checks and it was something of a relief to be anchored down by routine tasks. It gave her a solid base. Time went quickly, and she was surprised to find that nearly an hour had passed when Matthew unexpectedly put his head round the door as she was finishing with a patient.

'Would you strap up a foot for me?' he asked as she saw her patient to the door.

'Of course. What is it, a sprain?'

Before he had time to reply they were interrupted by the shrill ring of the phone and she went to answer it. Drew's voice came on the line, and it was a bit of a shock to hear him, so that she pulled in a quick breath. She hadn't thought about him in what seemed like ages, though it must have been only a couple of weeks since she'd last seen him. It was almost as if her life had undergone some kind of upheaval in that short time, and she couldn't think for a minute why that should be. Probably the move had altered her perception of things, she thought, frowning. Yes, that must be it.

'Hi, Becky, how are things? Have you settled in yet, at the house?'

'Yes, thanks.' She was surprised to hear from him in

the afternoon. He'd helped her move her belongings to the new place, but she hadn't seen him since then, and she'd assumed that he'd been busy. Drew had his own business, dealing with computers and accessories, and he'd put all his energy into building it up over the last few years. She'd sometimes thought it meant more to him even than she did. 'Was there something you wanted?' she asked, conscious that Matthew was waiting.

'There's a lull in the office, and I just thought it was a while since we talked,' Drew said. 'I wondered how you were doing.'

'Fine,' she said. 'Just fine.' She hoped he wouldn't keep her long. It was awkward taking calls when she was at work, and she tried to discourage it, unless it was something urgent.

'I thought perhaps we might go out,' he ventured. 'Are you free this evening? We could have dinner together.'

'Oh, Drew, I'm sorry, I can't—not tonight. I'm taking Sophie over to see Gran. It's her birthday.'

There was a pause, then Drew said, 'Tomorrow, then? By the way, I wondered if you'd like a little writing bureau for your living room. It's one that my aunt had, do you remember it? You were always taken with it. She decided that she wanted the space and thought of you. I could bring it over tomorrow and then we could go out.'

'Tomorrow,' she said. 'Yes, that sounds like a lovely idea.'

'I'll pick you up about eight,' Drew said. 'We'll go to the Riverside Inn; you always liked it there. Do you remember last summer we went there nearly every week?'

'Yes, I remember,' she said softly, though she reflected almost guiltily that it was the sunshine and lazy days she recalled, rather than the time she'd spent with Drew. She heard Matthew move impatiently by the door and she said quickly, 'Look, Drew, I have to go; I'm in the middle of a clinic.' She put the receiver down a few seconds later and turned back to Matthew.

The cold blast from his green eyes hit her like an icy shower. 'If you've quite finished organising your private life Miss Laurens,' he said in a clipped tone, 'perhaps you could attend to my patient.'

'I'm sorry. Though I could hardly foresee that I would get a phone call, could I?' she retorted acidly. 'You, I suppose, never receive personal calls when you're on duty.'

His glance flicked coolly over her. 'Mr Gregory is waiting in the treatment room. He has a painful March fracture, and I expect he'll be relieved to have it strapped up.'

Becky watched him turn and go from the room. She ought not to let his attitude bother her, but she felt bad about things, all the same. It wasn't so easy to dismiss it out of hand. For a while, they'd been getting on quite well, and she'd thought their bad start might, perhaps, be forgotten. Now, though, in the space of just a few minutes, it was as if they had gone right back to square one. The atmosphere had frozen over and she was left feeling distinctly chilled and thoroughly dejected.

CHAPTER THREE

'SHOULDN'T you be getting a move on?' Sophie clattered into the living room one morning as Becky sat, pen in hand, ostensibly going through her timetable for the day. 'You'll be late for work if you sit at that writing desk much longer.'

'I was just checking my diary,' Becky said, reluctant to admit that she'd been miles away, her thoughts taken up with the problem that had been occupying her these last few weeks—Matthew Kingston, or rather her working relationship with him.

They hadn't made a particularly good start, and his manner towards her remained coolly professional. That troubled her, she admitted, but why? Was it that she had hoped for something more? The errant thought filled her with self doubt. He was just a colleague, wasn't he? So why did she find herself thinking about him so much?

True, he worked tremendously hard, and he was unstinting in the time and effort he put into making sure that every aspect of his dealings with his patients ran smoothly, but she had come to learn that there was a very different side to him from the efficient professional man, that he had a good sense of humour along with a sensitive approach, which was what made him such a likeable man. That was probably why the patients had taken to him and felt prompted to ask to see him on repeat visits.

'You're dropping me off at Stacey's house this morning,' Sophie reminded her. 'I want to be there early, so we've time to talk before school.'

'I know. Just give me a minute to get my things together.' It was definitely time to stop wool gathering and turn her mind to more practical matters. Closing the diary, Becky pushed it into her roomy leather bag and stood up, closing the bureau.

It had been good of Drew's aunt to think of her when she'd wanted to dispose of this beautiful piece of furniture, and Becky hoped she'd shown her just how appreciative she was, making a point of going to see her armed with a box of chocolates as a thank you gesture.

The situation with Drew was slightly more tricky, and was beginning to bother her a little. He wanted to take her to the theatre, and she was pleased enough about that, but not so happy that he expected her to fit in instantly with his own plans as the fancy took him. More and more just lately that had been grating on her. He simply couldn't understand why she didn't immediately drop everything and agree to his suggestions.

There was Sophie to consider—surely he ought to realise that? Now, more than ever, she was responsible for her sister, and she'd feel much more relaxed and happy about going out with him on a night when she knew Sophie was spending an evening with friends. She'd tried to explain that, but you'd have thought she was talking another language, judging by his reaction. At least she'd persuaded him to wait until Sophie's next disco night, but it had been a grudging agreement, and what was the betting he'd bring it up again when she saw him tonight?

She heaved a sigh. Throughout their relationship, it had been the same story, but why did it have to be like that? Why couldn't he see things from her point of view? He seemed to be so blinkered, that was the trouble, but then, Drew had always wanted her to himself, had resented her other commitments, and she had to take a firm stand at some point or he would try to control her life completely.

'Aren't you ready yet?' Sophie wanted to know. Her overstuffed school bag was hanging from her shoulder, jerking precariously as she shifted from one foot to another, impatient with having to wait.

Becky reached for her coat. 'You're in a hurry,' she said. 'Is something special going off today?'

'I just want to make sure I have time to talk to my friends before registration. We need to sort out what we're doing tonight.'

'Oh, of course, you're going back to Stacey's house for an hour or so, aren't you?' Becky remembered. 'What's to sort out?'

'Nothing you'd understand,' Sophie said irritably.

Becky studied her for a second or two. 'I thought you were going to listen to records, try out make-up—that kind of thing.'

Sophie shrugged. 'Yes, we are, but I want to see what records they've brought. We might swap; we just want to get there early for a change. Does it matter? Can't you get a move on, Becky?'

Becky hid a grin. Girl talk, that must be it. 'OK, I shan't be a minute; I just want to go up to the bathroom and get some hand cream. You can go and wait in the car if you like.'

She ran upstairs to the bathroom and grabbed the tube of cream from the medicine cabinet. Then, just as she was about to lock it up again and go downstairs, she saw that Sophie's blood-glucose meter still sat on the glass shelf. Thoughtfully, she picked it up, along with the small bottle of reagent strips.

A few minutes later she slid in behind the wheel of her car and handed the kit to Sophie.

'You forgot these,' she said, and Sophie scowled.

'I don't see why I have to do so many blood tests,' she said with a heavy frown. 'They're pointless. I feel perfectly well, it's just a waste of time. Anyway, I'll be going to the clinic in a couple of weeks.'

'Even if you do feel all right,' Becky told her, 'you can't be sure your blood glucose levels are OK without

doing the tests.' She glanced at Sophie as she turned the
key in the ignition. 'What is it that bothers you most?'
she asked, but Sophie just lifted her shoulders, hunching
them disagreeably. 'Is it the actual finger-pricking that
bothers you?' Another shrug, and Becky was silent for
a moment, thinking. 'I know they're a nuisance,' she
said. 'I'm sure no one likes to do them day after day.'

'It isn't that,' Sophie said, cross now. 'Leave it, will
you? I don't want to talk about it.'

'No one will see the kit if you push it down in your
bag,' Becky persisted. 'And there must be somewhere
you can do the testing in private.' But she wasn't getting
through to her, she could see that, and she had to be
satisfied that Sophie at least pushed the things down into
a pocket of her bag. They didn't talk much for the rest
of the journey, and after she had dropped Sophie off at
her friend's house Becky drove on to the health centre,
her mind still preoccupied.

Some minutes later, she walked through to Reception
and saw that Matthew was in there talking to Nick Tyler.
The sight of him made her pause for a moment. The two
men were laughing quietly about something and she was
struck by the way Matthew's features changed when he
was relaxed. There was a warmth about him, a glint in the
green eyes, an attractive slant to his well shaped mouth.

'Morning, Becky,' Nick said, and she nodded in their
direction.

'Morning.' She noticed that smile had gone from
Matthew's face, was replaced with a polite formality,
and, unexpectedly, that stung a little. Why couldn't he
show her just a fraction of the warmth that he gave so
generously to others? She tried to dismiss the small hurt,
turning her attention to the files that were laid out on the
counter. What did it matter what Matthew thought of her?

She collected the notes that she would need for her
morning's list and took them through to her own room,
placing them on the work surface. Then she took off her

coat and hung it up before going to check her shelves and set things out for the morning's work.

About five minutes later, Matthew came into the room. He was holding a folder and as he threw it down onto the table he murmured, 'I think this is one of yours. I seem to be one missing . . . Do you think you might have picked mine up by mistake?'

She checked the pile. 'It's possible,' she said. She was very conscious of his nearness, that he was close enough for her to catch the faint scent of his cologne and feel the warmth emanating from his long, lean body as he watched her. He only had to stand by her side and her skin began to tingle and her temperature rocketed, and that was confusing; she didn't know why she was so aware of him as a man. She'd never been so tuned into anyone before, not even Drew. It made her jumpy whenever she was with him, made her feel as though she ought to put some distance between them, if only out of a sense of sheer self-preservation.

'Is this the one?' she asked, handing him a file. 'I don't recognise the name.'

'That's the one,' Matthew said. 'You obviously had your mind on something else when you picked these up.'

'Then again, it could have been put in the wrong pile to begin with,' she returned coolly, not altogether sure whether his tone held mild censure but determined to counteract it, all the same. 'Anyway, I dare say I would have noticed the file name soon enough.'

His mouth twisted briefly at her defensive reaction, a faint trace of amusement in his glance, but he said nothing and went from the room. He seemed to have a habit of leaving her feeling unsettled and on edge. It was thoroughly disturbing, the way he affected her, but whatever the reasons behind it she didn't have time to dwell on it now—there were patients waiting to be seen, and she had to pull herself together and get on with the day's work.

Her list was a long one, and she worked her way steadily through it, pleased that the rest of the morning seemed to be going smoothly, without too many hitches. There were a number of minor dressings to be dealt with and sutures to be removed before she could start the well-woman clinic. Then she took a number of smears, checked urine samples and blood pressures.

Jennifer Tynsdale, a slim girl in her early twenties, came into her room looking pale and anxious, and Becky said quietly, 'How are you, Jenny? Any problems you wanted to talk about?'

Jenny bit her lip, hesitating, then said jerkily, 'I wanted to ask you—I think I can feel some lumps—in my breasts—I don't think they were there a few weeks ago, and I'm...well...I'm a bit worried...' Her voice trailed off.

'I'll take a look, shall I?'

'Would you?' The girl looked relieved. 'I've been thinking about coming in for a few days, trying to pluck up courage, but Dr Lancaster's list's full this morning, apparently...and anyway, I didn't want to take up her time when I might just be fussing over nothing...'

Becky frowned. 'If something's worrying you, you should never be afraid to talk to one of the doctors about it. But I'm glad you felt able to come to see me. I can always arrange for you to see Dr Lancaster, if need be,' she added reassuringly. 'Just slip off your sweater and blouse for me, and lie down on the couch, and we'll see what we're dealing with. Do you examine your breasts regularly?'

'Not really—only when I think about it. I suppose I ought to...'

'Once a month is probably a good idea—when your period has finished might be a good time. You could check them when you're relaxed—in the bath, if you like.' Becky examined her carefully, and asked, 'Are you on the Pill?'

'Yes.' Jenny looked anxious again. 'Is something wrong?'

'I was just asking because women react in different ways to different kinds of contraceptive pills. Sometimes they can cause this kind of general lumpiness, but it isn't usually anything to worry about. It may be simply a matter of changing the pill for another kind, or occasionally it's suggested that a woman comes off it altogether. But you need to see the doctor so that she can advise you properly.' She smiled. 'You can get dressed again now, Jenny. I'll see if I can arrange for you to see Dr Lancaster this morning.'

While Jenny was dressing, she phoned through to Reception. 'You're in luck,' she told her a minute or two later. 'The doctor will see you in half an hour, when she's finished her appointments.'

'Thanks. I'm glad I came, after all. It was good of you to see me.'

'Any time. Whenever you're worried about anything at all, just come along and talk to me.' Becky saw her to the door, and was surprised to see Matthew heading towards her room.

He glanced around the empty waiting area. 'Is this a quiet moment for you? I saw a patient leaving just now.'

'I've a few minutes before the next appointment. Did you want me for something?'

'I wondered if you would have time to do an ECG on Mrs Forrest for me? She's complaining of chest pain and I want to eliminate a few possible causes.'

'Of course—I'll do it now.' She frowned, her mind flicking back over the patient's history. 'Mrs Forrest's a dear; she's been arthritic for a number of years, but there's never been any suggestion of a heart problem up to now.'

'I suspect the symptoms might be more related to her medication. I'll send her in to you, shall I? I'll come and look at the result after I've seen my next patient.'

'OK.' She went back into her room and got things ready, so that when Mrs Forrest arrived it took only a matter of moments to connect her to the machine and make the trace. 'All done,' she told her with a smile. 'You can go back and sit outside Dr Kingston's room.'

Mrs Forrest's eyes widened, her brows lifting in surprise. 'That was quick. I'd expected it to take a while.'

Becky shook her head. 'There's modern technology for you. . .just minutes, that's all.'

Matthew came to check the result a short time later, studying the trace thoughtfully. 'Good. No heart problem, then. She's probably suffering a spasm of the oesophagus. . .I expect it's down to the anti-inflammatories she's had to take over the years.'

'Isn't she taking something to counter any ill effects of those?' Becky queried. 'I thought she was prescribed tablets to protect the stomach lining when she started having problems?'

'She was, but she may not be taking them when she's supposed to, or she may need something to stop the acid completely. I'll talk to her about it.'

The receptionist came into the room just then, handing Becky an envelope. 'Someone left this at the desk for you, Becky. Didn't have time to wait.'

'Oh, thanks.' She took the envelope and studied it briefly, recognising Drew's handwriting. Why would he be sending her a note when she would be seeing him anyway this evening? Unless he couldn't make it for some reason. She pulled out the slip of paper as the door swung closed behind the girl, skimming the contents as she walked over to her desk.

Becky, I'm sorry but I shan't be able to make it this evening—a problem with one of my outlets. It's caused me a few difficulties and I shall have to go and sort it, which means I'll have to drive over there and

I shan't be back till late. Talk to you tomorrow.
Love, Drew.

'Love, Drew.' Such a small word, love, yet one with
such a wealth of meaning behind it. He'd scribbled it
casually, but she knew him well enough to know that he
cared about her, wanted to deepen their relationship. So
why didn't she feel anything when she read his note?
Anything other than. . .relief. Was that what she really
felt now that she knew she wouldn't be seeing him after
all? He must have dropped this note off as he was passing
by the centre. He'd obviously been in too much of a
hurry to stop and talk to her—just as well, perhaps, when
she was in the middle of a clinic. . .

'Is anything wrong?' Matthew's voice intruded on her
thoughts, and she tore her glance from the paper.

'Wrong? Oh. . .no, it's nothing— Ouch.' Her leg made
painful contact with the corner of a box of supplies that
had been delivered an hour or so ago, and she hopped
backwards, dropping the note onto her table and bending
to grasp her injured shin bone with one hand.

'I felt that for you,' Matthew said, grimacing in
sympathy. 'Let me take a look.'

'I'll be fine,' she got out through clenched teeth.
'It's nothing. Serves me right for not looking where I
was going.'

'I'll decide whether you're all right or not,' he said.
'Stand still. . . In fact, it would be better if you took off
your tights and sat down, so I can put a cold compress
on it. From the crack you gave it, I expect you'll end up
with a lump there the size of an egg.'

'I'm not wearing tights,' she muttered, and felt his
glance sear her legs.

'Stockings, then.' His mouth tilted in a way that
brought hot colour to her cheeks. 'Come on, Becky, do
as you're told.'

'No way,' she said, getting uptight at the very thought. 'I told you, I'll be just fine.'

He tutted at that, pushing her gently but firmly down into a chair, and then crouched down beside her, his large hand sliding around the swell of her calf and resting there. His touch did strange things to her, sent a wave of heat right through her, from her toes to the top of her head, making the blood pound in her ears. She met his glance, her thoughts spinning dizzily through a haze of burning sensation that had nothing whatever to do with the knock she'd had, and everything to do with the way his long, capable fingers were smoothing lightly over her skin.

'As I thought,' he murmured, 'you'll have a nasty bruise there. It's already swelling. Let's see if a cold pad of lint will help.' He stood up and went over to the sink, leaving her to gather her scattered wits as best she could. Her whole body seemed to have lit up in response to the glide of his hand, and it was a thoroughly unsettling reaction. She'd never felt like this before—never, not even with Drew. It was as though her hormones had suddenly gone crazy.

Matthew came back to her, kneeling down and wrapping a cold, water-soaked lint pad around her leg. That, at least, went halfway to bringing her back to normal. Even so, she found herself actually enjoying the feel of his hands on her flesh—not just enjoying but wanting more, wondering what it would be like if . . .

What was she thinking? Tiny beads of perspiration broke out on her brow, her mouth felt suddenly dry. It wouldn't do to go on sitting here like this, prey to the images her fevered imagination was conjuring up. Where was her loyalty to Drew? Surely it couldn't just disappear in a cloud of steam?

'I don't think you need do that any more,' she said, as evenly as she could manage, striving to inject a detached coolness into her voice. 'I'm fine now. It doesn't hurt any longer, and I really should be getting on with my clinic.'

He shot her a quick, narrowed glance, but without another word he removed his hand from her leg and got lithely to his feet, tossing the lint pad into a nearby bin.

'Then I'll leave you to it. It might be as well to get the van driver to stack deliveries somewhere less obtrusive next time—perhaps they could go in the vestibule or at the end of the corridor, where they're less likely to cause an accident.' He pushed the box out of the way and headed for the door, leaving her feeling unaccountably out of sorts.

Had she been too distant in her manner towards him? Why on earth couldn't she get it right, instead of rocketing from one extreme to the other? She was altogether too conscious of him, that was the trouble—so much so that it was affecting her judgement, making her behave in a less than natural way whenever he was around.

She went on with the morning's work, doing health checks where necessary, soothing the fears of a girl with an abnormal smear, and doing a pregnancy test for another. Calling in the next patient, a fair-haired, thin-looking woman, she invited her to sit down. 'Mrs Trent, is that right?'

'Yes.' She was quietly spoken, around her mid-thirties, and she appeared to be weary, her expression blank. There was a pale, anaemic look about her, Becky thought as she went to prepare the injection that had been noted down on her appointments list.

'Do you have a form with you from the doctor or the hospital?' she asked, looking through her paperwork. 'I don't seem to have one here for you.'

'I've got one somewhere,' Mrs Trent replied. 'It's probably in my bag. I'll see if I can find it for you.'

Becky was busying herself with the syringe when Matthew walked into the room. His coolness was almost palpable, she thought—such a contrast to his earlier

mood, though he could simply be deep in thought, preoccupied. He nodded towards the patient, obviously
recognising her, because he said wryly, 'You'll soon be
getting used to these, won't you?'

The woman nodded, grimacing a fraction. 'Too true.'

'Was there something you wanted?' Becky asked him,
placing the still packaged syringe on the table.

'Some paperwork I needed,' he answered, going over
to the filing cabinet. He was frowning as he pulled open
a drawer, glancing back at the table and the patient seated
there. 'Is that for Mrs Trent?' he asked, gesturing in the
direction of the syringe and the small phial that Becky
had placed next to it.

'That's right.' Becky stared at him, puzzled, wondering what had prompted him to ask.

He removed the paper he had been searching for, then
said briefly, 'Perhaps you would wait a moment before
carrying out the treatment? May I use your computer for
a second or two? There's something I want to check on.'

Becky wondered why she should have to postpone her
work, but she said simply, 'Help yourself,' and went
back to her patient, who was still searching in her bag
for the form.

'I'm sure I put it in here,' Mrs Trent said. 'I always
carry everything around with me—that's why my bag
weighs a ton and the strap keeps breaking.'

Becky smiled, but just then Matthew beckoned and
she looked at him questioningly. A muscle flicked briefly
in his jaw, and it occurred to her fleetingly that even
when his mood was indecipherable there was a lean,
sculpted quality to his features that tugged at the senses.
'Could I have a word with you for a moment, in private?'
His tone was brisk and businesslike, and something
about it made her feel oddly uneasy. Had she done
something wrong?

'Of course.' At odds with herself, she felt the spas-
modic thud of her pulse as she turned back to her patient

and said, 'Excuse me for just a moment, would you, Mrs Trent? I'll be back soon.'

She followed Matthew to his room, standing silent and waiting as he shut the door firmly.

He came abruptly to the point. 'Have you dealt with Mrs Trent before?'

She shook her head. 'No, I haven't had occasion to. Someone else ran the clinic before there was a change in the duty rota.'

'That's what I thought. She comes here once a month to have blood tests. Is that what you were intending to do this morning?'

'Well, no,' Becky answered. 'I have her listed for an injection.'

'Then perhaps you should check the details of her treatment,' Matthew said grimly, 'before you go ahead and do something you might have cause to regret.'

'I don't understand what you mean—' Becky began.

'I'm sure you don't,' he remarked tersely. 'In fact, you don't seem to be functioning properly at all today, if this morning's anything to go by. It won't do, Becky, you can't afford to have your mind on other things when you're dealing with patients.'

The criticism stunned her. 'I think there must have been a mistake of some sort—'

'There certainly has.' Matthew moved over to his desk and stabbed the computer keyboard, bringing up Mrs Trent's file. 'Can you see an injection listed anywhere?'

Becky felt ice-water flood her veins. 'Well, no,' she said, 'but—'

'But nothing,' Matthew cut in abrasively. 'You were about to inject my patient when in fact she should be receiving a blood test. What's the matter with you today?' His jaw clenched spasmodically. 'Are you having trouble with the boyfriend? Is that it?' His green eyes bored into her with. . .what was it?. . .contempt?

But this wasn't the time to start wondering about his

opinion of her, and, besides, his attitude was thoroughly unjustified.

'My private life is none of your business,' she retorted, stung.

'It is if it interferes with your work here.' His features were taut, his mouth making a hard line, and despite her need to put up a strong front her heart sank. Would she be forever damning herself in his eyes?

She frowned, anxiously trying to sift through what might have brought about this turn of events. 'I don't know how this has come about,' she said as calmly as she was able, 'but I'm sure she was on my list for an injection. I have to check.'

'I think you had better.'

He was icily remote as she walked from the room, but at least he hadn't slated her in front of anyone—she could be thankful for that. Even so, she was feeling disastrously shaky, and it took an effort to compose herself as she went to check the schedule.

With a trembling finger, she ran down the list of patients once more and found Mrs Trent's name. She was clearly marked down for an injection, and that knowledge alone ought to have made her feel some small relief that she hadn't made a mistake after all. But someone else definitely had—the person who made the appointment, perhaps? From the looks of things, it had been noted down wrongly, entered in the wrong book.

Becky pulled in a deep breath. Matthew was right, of course, the mistake shouldn't have been made in the first place, but at least she could feel secure in the knowledge that it wasn't her mistake. She'd find out exactly how it had come about when she had time to spare later on.

She walked back to her room and said, 'Sorry to keep you waiting, Mrs Trent. Have you managed to find your form?'

The woman nodded, handing over the blood-test form, and Becky started her preparations over again, this time fetching the tourniquet and the appropriate syringes.

She was relieved when the morning was over. Going to Reception to check on how the mistake had come about, she recognised the woman from the hardware store, Helen Mason, coming from Sarah Lancaster's room.

'You made an appointment, then,' Becky said, with a smile. 'I'm glad.'

'Oh, hello there. Well, yes, I thought I'd better take your advice, just to be on the safe side—the pain has been much worse lately. It's a problem with the sacro-something. . .I can't quite remember what Dr Lancaster said.'

'Sacroiliac?' Becky guessed. 'It's the lower part of your back, where it links with the hip.'

'That's it, yes. She showed me a model of the region and explained what was happening. She said I was having trouble with the muscles there, so you were right about that. She's given me a leaflet to explain what exercises I need to do to strengthen them—once the pain's gone. At least I have some stronger tablets to help deal with that, so I'm feeling a bit happier about things now.'

'That's good.'

After staying to chat for another minute or two, Becky went on her way through to Reception and had a word with the clerical staff. She didn't see Matthew again until the afternoon break, but when she entered the staff lounge he was standing by the window, glancing through the pages of a medical magazine. He looked tall and vigorously fit, the broad shoulders emphasised by the well cut lines of his suit jacket. He was a man totally in command of himself, seemingly relaxed, yet controlled and constantly alert.

'I'm glad I found you in here,' she said, thankful that they were alone in the room. His cool stare might have made her nervous at any other time, but she was set on putting the situation right, and she wasn't going to let his detached manner undermine her confidence in any way. 'I just wanted to say that I'd sorted out the problem this morning. The patient's name had been put down on the wrong list—but not by me,' she inserted hastily. 'I believe we had a temp on switchboard when the appointment was made, and she picked up the wrong treatment book.

'In any case,' she added, 'there wouldn't have been a problem, because I always do a safety check. I always ask for forms and I always check with the patient before carrying out any procedure.' She used a level tone as she battled to keep her emotions in check. 'You were right to be concerned, I grant you, but I think you were too ready to judge me. You automatically assumed I'd done the wrong thing.'

He put down the magazine and studied her, his dark brows edging together. 'I thought you were about to do something that might have dangerous consequences. If I seemed too quick in my judgement, it's because I have my patients' safety at heart. We owe them one hundred per cent and more, and when I see mistakes about to happen it makes me feel very concerned. I'm sorry if I misjudged you but, if you can see things from my point of view, it looked as though you'd already made one mistake this morning, with the files, and were about to make another. Appearances can be deceptive, I admit.'

'I just thought that you might have put some trust in me, that you might rely on me to do my job properly,' she retorted stiffly. She still felt the wounds from this morning's altercation; she'd been hurt, her confidence had taken a knock, and she wasn't ready to forgive him just like that.

'It isn't quite as simple as that, though, is it?' Matthew queried. 'You're not an open, easy-to-read person, are you? You keep yourself to yourself.'

Becky frowned at him. 'I don't know how you've managed to form that opinion,' she said tautly.

'Don't you? For most of the time since I came to this practice, you've been reserved and distant, putting up barriers. . .' His glance narrowed on her. 'But perhaps we made a bad start.'

She was stunned that he could feel that way. Did he really think she was reserved? But she *had* been on the defensive around him much of the time—she'd felt that she'd been at a disadvantage from the moment they'd met. Even so. . .

'Perhaps we did,' she admitted carefully. 'But that doesn't necessarily mean things are likely to change. You have to learn to accept me as I am.'

'So the wall stays firmly in place, does it?'

Becky shrugged. 'It wouldn't occur to you that you're the only one who thinks there's a problem, would it? I get on well enough with everyone else.'

Matthew eyed her shrewdly. 'That's true enough. Nick was singing your praises to me only this morning, telling me what a capable nurse you are, and how he'd like to persuade you to work with him in the asthma clinic.'

'He would?' A faint tension tightened the muscles between her shoulders, and she found herself wishing that Matthew might have a similar faith in her. What did she have to do to prove herself to him? And why should she care so much what he thought? 'He's seemed to be managing well enough with the staff he's had with him over the last months, since his wife left to do her health-visiting course. I know it's hard for anyone to live up to her standards; they made such a good team. He hasn't asked me to help out, though. . .not directly, anyway.'

'Nick's a very perceptive man. It could be that he guesses there are reasons you're avoiding it.'

Becky sucked in a deep breath, her mouth making an odd grimace. 'It's no big secret,' she said. 'My mother died after an asthma attack, and I don't think I could work so closely with patients who suffer in the same way. . .not right now, anyway.'

He let out a long, slow breath. 'I'm sorry,' he murmured, compassion filling his eyes. 'I can understand how you must feel. Did it happen recently?'

'Not exactly. It was about six years ago. I suppose that isn't recent, but it still hurts.'

'I can imagine that it would. But there could be another way to deal with the situation, you know. Haven't you ever thought that working with other asthmatics would help you feel you're doing something to stop other people suffering the way your mother did?'

She bit her lip. 'It's possible, I suppose, but I don't think I'm ready for it yet. It would just bring back too many memories.'

Matthew studied her thoughtfully, his glance moving over the bright sheen of her hair and coming to rest on the vulnerable curve of her mouth. 'I can see how it might. Thank you for telling me, anyway. I know it must have been difficult for you.'

She nodded cautiously, quiet for a moment as she recalled the tension of the last few hours. The day had gone badly, and she didn't want to go on working with him in such a strained atmosphere. There had only ever been the one time when they'd had any real kind of rapport—when little Davey Jarrom had been brought into the surgery by his mother and Matthew had sent him to hospital. That seemed such a long time ago, though, and it wouldn't do to keep thinking back. Life had to move on. Going over to the door, she said, 'I suppose I'd better get back to work, or I shall have a full waiting room.'

He inclined his head briefly, his gaze watchful as she crossed the room. 'Me too.'

At the door, she turned and said, 'I've been meaning to ask. . .the little boy, Davey, the one with meningitis. . . have we heard anything about him lately? He should be home by now, shouldn't he? But I thought I heard his name mentioned this morning in Reception.'

'As a matter of fact, I have to go and visit him when I finish here. Yes, he is at home. Apparently he's not well, though, and his mother put in a call to the surgery. In fact, I wondered—' He broke off.

'You wondered?' Becky prompted.

'I wondered if I could persuade you to come along with me on my calls this evening. I'm not familiar with the area where the Jarroms live, but I heard that you come originally from that part of the county, and you could maybe point me in the right direction. It's quite isolated around there, but you might know some of the local landmarks. Besides that, the little boy got on well with you and so did the mother.' He paused. 'Unless you have other plans for this evening?'

She'd been thinking about what she might do since Drew had cancelled. 'None that I can't change.' She grinned at him. 'I was going to strip the living-room walls and get on with the decorating, but that can wait. I've worked my way through the other rooms and I could do with a break. Besides, I'd like to see the little boy again; I was worried about him. But I'll need to drop my car off at home first.'

'That's OK. I'll pick you up from there.'

It was dark when they started out. The Jarroms lived in what had once been a farmhouse on land which had then been divided up and sold off for development. The house was at the end of a long, winding track full of potholes that needed to be negotiated carefully, and although Matthew drove slowly it was a bumpy ride, and Becky found herself thrown against him on more than one occasion.

The unexpected contact had a stunning effect on her, heightening her already charged senses so that she had to curl her fingers to stop them from trembling. She tried not to think about the effect his strong male presence had on her. That was treading on dangerous ground, making her aware of sensations she had never experienced before. It was too much, too nerve-racking, and she had to find a way of dealing with the alarming emotions he stirred in her whenever he was close.

Mrs Jarrom answered their knock at the door, looking harassed. In the background they could hear sounds of a child wailing miserably.

'Come in, will you? I'm sorry about the noise. He's been like this all day on and off. I just don't know what to do with him. I thought he was over the meningitis, but he still doesn't seem well.'

'Let's have a look at the little lad,' Matthew said. In the living room Davey sat on a rug, surrounded by toy cars and trucks, and at the sight of Becky and Matthew he set up an even louder wail than before.

'Shush, Davey,' his mother said. 'It's all right, it's the doctor and the nurse come to see you.'

'No like hospital,' Davey complained. 'No like it.'

'I don't like hospitals either,' Becky said, and the boy was surprised enough to look at her curiously. 'You look nice and cosy here,' she went on. 'Look at all these cars. My goodness, there are lots of them. I bet Dr Kingston's never seen such a wonderful collection before.'

Davey surveyed his fleet and Matthew moved next to him, going down on his haunches to be nearer the boy's level. 'You've even got a tipper truck,' he said. 'I bet Teddy wouldn't mind a ride in that.' He looked at the huge teddy bear sitting on the floor beside them.

Davey chuckled at that. 'He's too big!' he exclaimed.

'Is he? Well, I never,' Matthew said, looking surprised. 'Ah, well, perhaps Teddy doesn't want a ride anyway. Has he been poorly like you?'

Davey nodded. 'He's hurting,' he said.

'Is he? Where does he hurt?' Matthew asked, and Davey picked the teddy bear up and examined him thoughtfully.

'Here,' he said, pointing to Teddy's ear.

'We'd better take a look.' Matthew opened his case and took out his auriscope, shining the light into Teddy's ear. 'It must hurt him quite a lot,' he murmured. 'We'll have to make him better, won't we? Shall we put some drops in his ears?'

Davey nodded slowly and watched intently as Matthew made a pretence of putting a dropper to the teddy's fur. When he'd finished, Matthew said, 'There, he'll soon feel better now. What about you? Are you hurting anywhere? Shall I have a look and see what's causing the trouble?'

Davey nodded again, and allowed Matthew to examine his ears gently. 'Oh, that looks uncomfortable.' Matthew made a sympathetic grimace. 'I bet that's been hurting. Could I look in your mouth as well?' Gently, he coaxed the little boy into letting him examine him properly, and when he'd finished he said, 'I think we'll have to give you some drops as well as Teddy. I'll give Mummy a prescription so that she can get you some from the chemist.'

'Mummy get drops,' the boy agreed, nodding solemnly. 'Make Davey better.'

Matthew turned to Mrs Jarrom. 'I think I've found the cause of the trouble,' he said. 'It looks like a problem in the middle ear but it should clear up in a few days.'

'Thank heaven for that,' Mrs Jarrom sighed in relief as she took the prescription he handed her. Davey was pretending to put drops in Teddy's ears and they waved and left him to it, walking towards the door. 'I was dreading that he'd have to go back into hospital,' she added. 'He really didn't like it in there...they gave him a lumbar puncture and he had a drip in his arm. I just hated to see him like that.'

'I'm sure he'll get over it soon enough. He should be fine in a day or so, but if there's any problem just give us a ring at the surgery.' Matthew smiled at the woman as she held open the door.

'It's so difficult to know what to do for the best sometimes. I don't want to be one of those mothers who fuss
unnecessarily, but you can never quite tell with children
whether it's serious or not.'

'I'm sure no one's going to say that you're fussing,
Mrs Jarrom. It's natural to worry. . .we just have to try
and keep things in proportion, that's all.'

The next call was to a man suffering from aching
joints, along with shivers and bouts of fever, and Matthew
put the stethoscope to his chest, listening carefully before
straightening up and saying, 'It's flu, I'm afraid, so you'll
need to stay in bed for a day or so. Your lungs are a
bit congested, so I think you'd better have a course of
antibiotics, and you can take paracetamol for the aches
and pains. It'll help bring your temperature down
as well.'

Their final visit of the evening took them along a
country lane to a row of terraced cottages on the outskirts
of a village. Matthew knocked at a door in the middle
of the block, and they waited a while until they heard
shuffling footsteps within.

An elderly woman opened the door, pulling it slowly
back and standing to one side. 'Are you the doctor? I've
not seen you before. Oh, you've brought Becky along
with you—that's all right, then. You'd better come in,
both.' She was painfully thin, her features gaunt, the skin
stretched over hollowed cheeks.

Matthew took her arm, gently guiding her back to the
sitting room. 'Becky's come to help me find my way
about. Otherwise I might have been wandering these
villages for the next hour or so.'

'What have you been doing, my love?' Becky asked
softly, studying her frail figure with affection. 'Have you
been getting up to mischief again?'

'Who, me? Chance'd be a fine thing!' Victoria
Kirkwood chuckled, her body shaking with the action.
'No, it's just that I passed out and banged myself again.

My arm's just bruised, that's all. I wouldn't have bothered you with it; it was her next door insisted on calling you out. Let me get you a cup of tea. . .'

'I'll do it,' Becky said. 'I know my way about the kitchen. You sit and talk to Dr Kingston.'

She heard them chatting as she set out cups and filled the pot. It soon became pretty clear that Victoria hadn't been eating well just lately, despite her protests to the contrary, and Becky saw that there was hardly any food in the cupboards, which meant she probably hadn't felt up to doing much shopping. That probably accounted for the blackouts she'd been having.

'We can arrange meals on wheels for you,' Matthew told her, 'and we could get a home help to come in every day.'

The idea was firmly squashed. 'I'm not having anyone coming here nosing about. I shall manage well enough.'

'But you need to eat,' Matthew insisted as he examined the injured arm. 'Something more than you have been doing up to now. These fainting spells aren't going to go away unless you get something substantial inside you—and you know how fragile your bones are. Last time you fell you fractured your wrist. We don't want that to happen again, do we? You've been lucky this time—just a nasty sprain.'

'I get by all right, without any interference. If I let you take over now, next thing, you'll be sending me off to live in a home. No, I'm just fine as I am.'

'No one's suggesting that you leave here, Victoria,' Becky put in, setting the tray down on a table. 'But a bit of help about the place would be nice, wouldn't it? A hot meal once a day wouldn't be that much of an intrusion, and you'd probably feel much better able to cope.'

'Well, maybe. . . Just a dinner, mind you; I'm not agreeing to anything else.'

Becky watched, absorbed, as Matthew fixed a sling in

place to make the arm more comfortable and wrote out a prescription for painkillers for the wrist, which was still giving her trouble. He was so tender with her, his fingers remarkably deft, and it was hard to drag her gaze away from him. When he had finished, they drank the tea and chatted for a few minutes more before they decided it was time to leave.

Becky walked quietly alongside him as they made their way back to the car. Sliding in behind the wheel, Matthew stretched, easing taut limbs.

'You look tired,' she said, quelling a sudden, almost irresistible urge to wind her arms around him and ease the frown from his brow.

'I was on call last night,' he told her, 'standing in for Martyn. It's been a long day. . . At the practice I'll be going to, they're trying a new system, operating a night service in conjunction with the local town and hospital. It means the patients don't get to see their own doctor at night—'

'But their own doctor will be much more bright-eyed and alert next day.'

'There is that, of course. I'm glad you came along tonight. Having you here with me has made all the difference. You were especially good with Mrs Kirkwood. Thanks, Becky.'

'She's a dear, and I was happy to come along.' She hesitated a moment. 'You haven't eaten yet, have you?' she guessed. On impulse, she told him, 'I've a casserole prepared at home. There should be plenty for two people; would you like to share it with me?' A sudden thought dropped into her mind like a stone. 'That is. . .' She'd never questioned that there might be anyone waiting for him. 'You're not married?'

He shook his head. 'I'm a restless spirit, always on the move, from one end of the country to another. Not exactly the ideal candidate for making a commitment,' he said wryly. 'What about you—would you be eating alone otherwise?' he asked, a dark brow edging upwards.

'Sophie's out tonight,' Becky explained. 'I forgot when I made the casserole. I'm not used to cooking for just one.'

Matthew's gaze drifted over her. 'Sophie?' he queried. 'Isn't that your sister?'

'That's right. She lives with me.'

'Ah. . .' There was a wealth of meaning in that single word. 'Then you don't live with the boyfriend,' he said, making it a statement of fact.

'I don't remember ever saying that I did,' she told him bluntly, and he laughed.

'You just wanted me to think that, in case I was an axe murderer or something.' His green eyes glittered with amusement.

'Or something,' she said, watching, in fascination, the way his features changed when he smiled.

She watched him again later as he cleaned up his plate. He had a good, healthy appetite, for all that there wasn't a spare ounce of flesh on him.

'That was delicious. Thank you,' he murmured, satisfaction curving his mouth, and her cheeks warmed at the compliment.

'I'm glad you enjoyed it. It's good to see a man eat with such relish. Do you cook for yourself?'

'More often than not. I'm a dab hand at steak and the occasional omelette, but I've had more microwave dinners than I care to remember. It made a pleasant change, sharing this with you. You'll have to let me return the gesture. A night out, perhaps? Dinner— tomorrow? We could take in a show.' He smiled at her and again she was struck by the clean lines of his features, the attractive tilt to his mouth and the warm gleam in his green eyes.

'That sounds good, but I've already made arrangements with Sophie for tomorrow.'

'The weekend, then?'

'Booked, I'm afraid.'

His eyes narrowed fractionally. 'A woman in demand. I'll have to do something about that.' His glance held a breathtaking mixture of threat and promise.

She felt a sudden rush of nervous energy charge her limbs. 'I think. . .I'll make coffee,' she said, scraping back her chair.

'You're trying to avoid me,' he said. 'I wonder why?' His hand brushed her arm, and warmth enveloped her, filled her body with leaping sensation. How had he guessed?

'You're imagining it,' she muttered. 'What reason would I have?' She busied herself with the coffee and heard him move behind her, collecting up dishes and placing them in the bowl at the sink, coming to stand beside her. It was then that the lights went out and the house was plunged into darkness.

'Oh—' She was flustered for a moment, unable to see anything in the blackness that had descended.

'Must be a power cut,' she heard him murmur. 'They were having trouble with the supply earlier today. Have you any candles?'

She tried to peer into the darkness and saw only shadows. 'In a drawer somewhere; I'll see if I can find them.' Cautiously, she took a few steps across the room, and felt the brush of his arm against hers. It was a reassuring, heated contact in a dark void, and the feel of his hard body against hers had an electricity all of its own, so that she almost expected the kitchen to light up in response.

Her lungs contracted. She wasn't thinking at all clearly, she realised, and struggled to pull herself together. 'Candles,' she muttered, and felt her way towards a cupboard. Pulling the drawer open with trembling fingers, she felt for the box of matches that lay alongside the candles and in the next moment Matthew had taken over, there was a rasp of a match and the flicker of flame casting strange shadows around the room. She set the lighted candle in its holder on the work surface and gave a faint sigh of relief. She hadn't realised until then that she'd been holding her breath.

'Are you all right?' Matthew asked quietly. 'Being flung into pitch-darkness like that can make you feel panicky.' His hands were reaching for her, turning her towards him, and she went into his embrace gladly, thankful for the comfort of his strong male presence and the reassuring thud of his heartbeat against her cheek.

A moment later, he bent his head towards her, and the touch of his mouth on hers was coaxingly warm and gentle. His arms folded about her, the kiss deepening, shocking her into startled response. She felt the softness of her curves crushed against him, felt the hard strength of his body as his palm flattened on the small of her back, urging her closer to him. Her limbs were weak, insubstantial as thistledown, her whole body yielding to the lure of his caressing hands. Heat surged through her veins, sent the blood pounding in her ears. For a wild, lingering moment, she was lost in a vortex of powerful sensations, her body alive with heart-racing excitement.

Then the power flickered back on, filling the kitchen with blinding white light. The suddenness of it made her gasp and for a while she lost all sense of time and place and simply stared up at him in shock.

'I didn't mean for that to happen,' he muttered. 'But once you were in my arms things seemed to spiral out of hand. . .'

Yes, that was how it had been for her too. She had lost all reason, given herself up to a tingling, mind-rending awareness that she'd never known before. . .not even with Drew.

Reality came back on the crest of a cold wave of acknowledgement. How could she have forgotten about Drew so easily?

Slowly she pulled away from him, ruthlessly denying

the magnetic tug of her senses. What on earth had she
been thinking of, clinging to him that way? She'd known
Drew for three years, and yet here she was, practically
going up in flames the moment Matthew touched her—
a man she'd known a mere fraction of that time, a man
who wouldn't even be staying in the area for more than
a month or so.

It was sheer madness. She'd always looked for commitment, a lasting relationship. She'd never gone in for
wild, brief affairs, least of all with someone she had to
work with every day in such a close community. Their
working relationship had been difficult enough, without
this to add complications.

'I wasn't thinking straight,' she mumbled, a little
raggedly. 'You said earlier, it's been a long day. . .and
well. . .when the lights went out, I was confused for a
while.' Her voice firmed as she took in a deep, steadying
breath. 'But I'm OK now, and I think perhaps you
should go.'

'We have to talk. . .'

She shook her head, her hand flattening on his chest
when he would have drawn her close again. 'It's late,'
she said. 'We're both tired, and it's for the best if you
go now.'

He looked down at her, his expression shuttered. 'If
that's what you really want.' His mouth twisted briefly.
'But you can't keep running for ever, you know.'

'I don't know what you mean. I'm not running from
anything, least of all you.'

'Aren't you?' His eyes were darkly mocking as he left
her and went to the door.

CHAPTER FOUR

'WILL Sophie be staying overnight at her friend's house?'

The curtains had closed on the first act and the theatre lights were brightening to a warm golden glow as Drew led the way through the mass of people all with the same aim in mind, heading upstairs for the refreshments at the interval.

'It seemed the best idea,' Becky murmured, sending him a sideways glance. He was a good-looking man, several inches taller than herself, with thick dark hair that framed strong features. 'The disco will be going on quite late, and Stacey's parents offered to pick the girls up afterwards.'

'So you'll be able to forget about her for a while.' His satisfaction showed in the hazel gleam of his eyes. 'It's about time you were able to concentrate on your own needs, instead of constantly having to look out for other people.'

Her mouth curved faintly with amusement. 'To hear you talk, anyone would think I had no life of my own.'

'You don't. For as long as I've known you, you've been acting as sister, mother, housekeeper, and heaven knows what else besides, as well as holding down a full-time job. You're still young; you should be able to put all that behind you and have fun, live a little.'

'I do have fun,' Becky protested mildly, 'and I'm perfectly content with the way things are,' but her comment slid past him as he concentrated on negotiating a path through the crowd towards a quiet corner. There was a table by a velvet-draped window with a couple of chairs left empty, and she sat down as he pulled out a seat for her, casting a glance about the comfortably furnished bar, listening to the chatter all around them.

'I'll go and find the drinks we ordered,' Drew said. 'When I get back, you can tell me all about the kind of week you've had.'

She wasn't so sure she wanted to dwell on that, because inevitably her world revolved around the health centre, and Matthew was an integral part of that. Thinking about him brought to mind disturbing images, and joltingly reminded her of the way things had gone rapidly out of control that night at her house.

Just one touch, that's all it had taken, and her temperature had sky-rocketed in a way that she'd never experienced before—it simply didn't bear thinking about... Recalling it now was enough to bring a flush of warm colour to her cheeks. That quick flare of attraction had taken them both by surprise, since it wasn't as though either of them was looking for any kind of involvement. She'd been perfectly content with her relationship with Drew up to now, hadn't she? It was easygoing, undemanding—at least on her part—and she'd accepted that this was what she wanted from life; she'd never thought herself the sort of person who could cope with a wild affair. Heaven forbid, there'd been enough uncertainty in her life so far, enough turmoil and upheaval, and Matthew was the very last person she should be thinking about. He was moving on, and if she had any sense at all she'd remember that.

It hadn't been easy working with him since that evening, trying to act as though nothing had happened, and she only hoped that no one at the centre had noticed the undercurrent of tension that sparked the atmosphere whenever they were in a room together. She'd find it hard to cope with people's curiosity.

Why was it so difficult to accept him simply as a colleague, like any other? It ought to be easy enough to work alongside him, but since he'd come on the scene

all kinds of conflicting emotions had stirred in her—
emotions she didn't want to have to deal with. Even now,
when she should be able to relax and enjoy the evening,
he was intruding on her thoughts in a profoundly
disturbing way.

She searched the room for sight of Drew, then sucked
in her breath with shocked surprise as her gaze fastened
on the very man she'd been trying to forget. Somehow,
she hadn't expected to see Matthew here, though she'd
once heard him say that he enjoyed going to the theatre
from time to time. His cool glance meshed with hers,
then, after a moment's hesitation, he detached himself
from the group he was with. He was coming towards
her. ..

He was wearing a dark, expensively cut suit, which
emphasised the breadth of his shoulders and made the
most of his long, lean frame. The sight of him made her
throat go dry and her pulse begin to thud in an alarming
fashion, and she found that her fingers were tightening
with a resurgence of the earlier tension. She prised them
open. No doubt he felt he had to be polite and acknowl-
edge her presence here, and she would have to do
likewise.

'This is a surprise,' Matthew said, his deep voice
smoothing over her nerve-endings and causing her heart
to make a funny little lurch against her ribcage. 'I had
no idea you intended coming here this evening. Are you
enjoying the play?'

'I am,' she said, making an effort to respond in a
casual fashion, and gratified that she managed to keep
an even tone. 'This is a real treat for me. It's a perform-
ance I've wanted to see for a long time.'

'Me too. Are you a regular theatre-goer?'

She gave a small laugh at that. 'Unfortunately, no. I
can't afford to come here as often as I'd like, but I do
have a friend who works in the green-room, and she gets
free tickets which she passes on to me occasionally.'

Matthew's green eyes flickered as his gaze met hers. 'You should have told me. I'd have brought you. If only I'd known—I might have broken down your resistance by simply dangling two tickets. Perhaps next time. . .' His grin was wicked, and she chuckled.

'You think I'd be such a pushover, don't you?'

His smile sent a flush of heat along her cheekbones, but his tone was even enough as he asked, 'Are you with your friend this evening?'

'No.' She paused. 'I came with Drew. He's gone to get drinks.'

His glance narrowed, flitting around the room, and to fill the brief moment of silence that had fallen she added, 'It's a crush in here, isn't it? You have to fight just to get near the bar.'

Even as she spoke, she saw that Drew was making his way back from there, and a fleeting moment of disappointment washed over her, before it was replaced by a small sense of shock. How could she be so disloyal? Drew approached the table and handed her a glass of wine. He frowned slightly as he saw Matthew.

Becky introduced the two men to each other. 'Matthew and I work together,' she told Drew. 'He specialises in diabetes care.'

'You two have something in common, then,' Drew said. 'I'm afraid I don't know about the medical side of things, so Becky doesn't get to bring her work home with her, so to speak. But perhaps that's a good thing in some ways.'

'Possibly,' Matthew agreed. 'Though, talking things through can be a good way to unwind. What work do you do?'

'I have my own business—computers and software.'

Becky glanced at Drew surreptitiously as he began to talk about his involvement. He was on solid ground here, and his enthusiasm for the subject showed in the way he gestured with his hands, in the fleeting curve of his mouth. Matthew listened to what he was saying, but she sensed a remoteness in him now. His earlier, relaxed manner had disappeared.

'It was hard work building things up initially, but now we're expanding all the time,' Drew went on.

She could vouch for all the effort he'd put in. She admired him for his determination to make a go of it, but she couldn't help feeling sometimes that in the three years she'd known him his particular interests had always come first and foremost. Her own problems seemed to get pushed into the background somehow, as if they weren't really all that important, and in Drew's perception of things that was probably true. For him, it was definitely a man's world, and she'd long since realised that he was an out and out chauvinist.

Matthew dragged her attention back to the present. 'I should go back and join my friends,' he said. 'They'll be wondering what's happened to me. I expect I shall see you at the centre tomorrow morning. It's your turn for the Saturday roster, isn't it?'

She nodded, faintly pleased that he'd remembered. 'It soon comes around, doesn't it? One in three.'

'Goodnight, then.' He inclined his head briefly towards Drew, and started to walk back to his companions. Becky watched him go, feeling oddly let down, though she couldn't imagine why that should be. He'd spent a courteous few minutes talking to them, because that was what might have been expected of him, and he'd taken an equally well-mannered leave of her. What more could she have hoped for? And what was she doing, anyway, letting her thoughts revolve around him so much?

'Perhaps now I can have you to myself,' Drew said, swallowing the contents of his glass and placing it back on the table. 'We get little enough chance to be alone with each other as it is, without having people descend on us out of the blue.'

She lifted a finely arched brow. 'You can hardly expect

to find privacy in a place like this. Besides, I see nothing wrong in his coming over to talk to us. I work with him, so it would have been strange if he'd ignored me.'

'That's just my point. You see him every day, you're with Sophie too, and your time's always taken up with something or other. I want you to myself for a change. Is that such a bad thing? I like being with you, Becky; you're soothing, relaxing to be around. I just wish we could spend more time together, just the two of us, without you constantly having to fit other people into your arrangements, especially Sophie. Is that really too much to ask?'

She frowned, picking up her glass and running a finger experimentally around the rim. 'I hadn't realised that it was such a problem for you—but perhaps that's because things have always seemed fine to me just the way they are. We both lead busy lives, and there are bound to be times when we have to make adjustments. You have your business to run, and I have Sophie to take care of. She's my responsibility; I have to take her into consideration when I'm planning things.' She sipped the wine slowly, feeling it ease the dryness of her throat.

Drew's lips compressed. 'But Sophie isn't going to be part of your life for ever, is she? Surely you should be thinking of yourself, of your own future?'

She blinked at that, and placed her glass carefully next to his on the table. 'Should I? Most of the time, I prefer to live each day as it comes. Of course I do think of the future, sometimes, but Sophie's always a part of it in some way or other. She's my sister, the only truly close family I have.'

'So you're going to put your life on hold, are you?' Drew said curtly. 'You're going to put Sophie first the whole time, regardless of what I feel, is that it?'

Becky stared at him, faintly shocked by his aggressive manner. 'Don't you think you're overreacting to the situation? Has it really seemed so bad?'

His hands moved in a dismissive gesture. 'Think about it from my point of view. There were times when we could have gone away for the weekend, but no, you had to stay to see to Sophie, you couldn't leave her. And then there were all those evenings when we couldn't be alone because Sophie was staying in, or because there were problems with her medication and you had to stay and sort it out. I want some kind of life with you, Becky, but you're asking an awful lot of me.'

'Am I?' She studied him with troubled eyes, trying to understand his grievances. 'I wasn't aware that I'd made any demands of you.' But then, a tiny voice sounded in her head, perhaps she hadn't really wanted to. Something had always held her back.

His mouth made a bitter grimace. 'It wouldn't be in your nature to do that, would it? But if we're to have any kind of future together something needs to be sorted out, and I don't think I'm being unreasonable in what I'm saying. No man wants to be saddled with a ready-made family.'

She swallowed hard. 'What was I supposed to do? What could I have done differently?' And, when it came down to it, did she want to change anything? He was talking about a future together, and it came as a shock now to find herself questioning that. Did she want a future with him?

The bell rang for the second act, and Drew said, 'Maybe she could have stayed overnight with her friends more often, or you could have simply left her to her own devices. She's old enough, surely?'

'I don't know.' She really didn't. Sophie had been the heart of her life these last few years, and thinking about that made her chew at her lip defensively. 'Perhaps I do worry too much, but I don't see how I can be any other way. She's been through a lot, losing our parents, being ill. She's vulnerable. She's not like any other teenager, in a secure family, with normal, everyday problems. I

hoped you'd understand that.' Shouldn't he understand?
Weren't her feelings every bit as important as his?

The bell rang again, and they left the rapidly emptying
bar to take their seats for the second half. She was
relieved that the subject was being dropped for the time
being, but it would surface again, sooner or later, and it
stayed in her mind, spoiling the rest of the evening.
Perhaps she was being unfair to him, expecting too much
of him, as he'd suggested, but if she was to feel at all
secure within herself she had to follow the dictates of
her conscience.

Drew took her home after the play had finished. They
didn't talk much on the journey, but when he eased the
car to a halt outside her house he turned towards her
with an expectant glance. He was taking it for granted
that she would invite him in for coffee, but a gulf had
come between them, and right now she wasn't at all sure
how to bridge it, or whether she even wanted to try.

'I want to get an early night,' she told him, knowing
that it was a lame excuse but needing time to herself. 'I
have to work in the morning.'

Her decision bothered him, she could see that, but she
hoped he wasn't going to try to persuade her to change
her mind. She was feeling prickly and on edge, and when
he reached for her she resisted. She didn't want him to
kiss her. He frowned, sitting back in his seat, his fingers
going to the wheel and restlessly twisting there.

'What's wrong with you?' he demanded. 'You're different tonight, somehow. I've never known you like this
before.'

'I need to be on my own. I need to think.'

'Why? What's there to think about?'

'Us,' she admitted on a level note. 'I don't think this
is working. I hadn't realised until now, but there are too
many problems.'

'Becky, you don't know what you're saying. We
should talk—'

'Not now, Drew. I'm tired. . .I'm sorry. . .' Turning away from him, she reached for the door.

'Is there someone else?'

She shook her head, getting out of the car and moving blindly towards the house. Someone else? Matthew's image formed in her mind, but she pushed it ruthlessly away. Matthew didn't want to get involved, did he? He wasn't cut out for commitment, he'd said; he was always on the move. That was how he preferred to live his life.

She heard Drew start up his car and accelerate away with an angry growl of the engine and a cloud of exhaust fumes.

She was almost ready for bed when the phone rang, and she stared at it for a moment, biting her lip. Was that him? Had he arrived home and decided that they needed to talk? She didn't want to talk to him, not right now, when she was still mulling things over in her head, when she was still so confused. The ringing went on, though, disturbing the peace of the night, and she walked across the room and lifted the receiver.

It wasn't Drew on the line, however; it was Stacey's mother and she sounded upset.

'Thank heaven you're home, Becky,' she said. 'I've been trying to reach you—I wasn't sure what time the play finished, and I needed to talk to you.'

'What's wrong?' Becky asked, alert and suddenly tense. 'Are the girls all right? Is it Sophie, has something happened?'

'It's Sophie,' Jane said, agitated. 'I didn't think she looked well when the girls came back from the disco, but she said she was all right and she was going to go up to bed. Then after half an hour or so Stacey came into our room. She said Sophie was being sick and that when she tried to talk to her she wasn't getting any sense out of her. She couldn't get her to answer properly, and then she just. . .well, she just collapsed. It was so frightening.'

'I'll come over,' Becky said quickly.

'No—we couldn't rouse her, so we've called an ambulance, and they're taking her to the hospital now. It would be quicker for you to go straight there. I'm sorry, Becky. . .if there's anything at all that I can do, just let me know.'

Becky absorbed the news with a cold sense of shock. 'I'll go there now,' she said. 'Thanks, Jane, for letting me know.' Her mind was racing as she broke off the call. If they hadn't been able to rouse her, then it probably wasn't a hypoglycaemic attack, because she'd have come out of that within a few minutes.

She threw on her clothes and rushed out to the car. The roads were clear in the early hours of the morning, and she drove to the hospital as fast as she dared, her fingers gripping the wheel, her whole body taut with stress. All her professional calm had deserted her now, when she most needed it. None of her training helped. How could it, when this was Sophie?

Sophie was still in a coma when Becky walked onto the ward, and Becky's heart seemed to twist in a spasm of pain as she looked down at her sister lying in the hospital bed, her brown hair fanning out on the pillow, a stark contrast to the white linen. She looked so pale and helpless.

'We've put in a nasogastric tube so that she doesn't inhale any vomit,' the nurse told her. 'I know it doesn't look very nice but it's not as bad as it seems.' She gave Becky a reassuring smile.

'I know,' Becky said quietly. 'I'm a registered nurse.' She looked at the intravenous infusion of saline and dextrose, and knew that there would be a catheter in place too, so that they could do urine tests while Sophie remained unconscious. The oscilloscope was there to detect cardiac arrhythmias, and the charts at the end of the bed were being updated so that the insulin doses could be worked out according to the blood-glucose levels. Everything was being done that should be done. She just had to let them get on with it.

'Do you know anything about how she came to be in this state?' she asked. 'I came here in such a rush, I didn't think to find out.'

'It looks as though she's missed an insulin injection. Has she done that before, do you know?'

Becky shook her head. 'I don't always check. I thought she had enough common sense to realise—' She broke off, battling with the sudden sting of tears. 'I tried to tell her how important it is.'

'It happens,' the young nurse said. 'She's at that age, isn't she? When she comes out of this, perhaps it will have taught her a lesson. Do you want to stay with her for a while? There's a machine at the end of the corridor where you can get a coffee or tea, if you'd like.'

'Thanks,' Becky said. 'I'll just sit here by the bed.'

'We'll be in and out all the while. Make yourself comfy.'

Becky nodded and carefully took a seat at the side of the bed, all at once aware that her limbs were shaky. She was overwhelmed by a feeling of loneliness that was like nothing she'd ever felt before. Even after her mother and father died, she'd not experienced such a depth of isolation.

'You have to get better, Sophie,' she whispered. 'You must.' There was no response and she hadn't expected any, of course. It was just a question of waiting now, but, much as she tried to keep a professional view of the situation, it was hard to stay calm. She wanted to be doing something but she didn't want to get in the way. At first her stomach tightened every time anyone came into the room, but after a while she became oblivious to the comings and goings of the nursing staff.

If only there was someone she could talk to, someone

to share her feelings with. Oddly, her thoughts turned to Matthew, and she imagined the strength of his arms around her, how it would feel to be comforted by him. If only he could be here with her now.

The thought swamped her with such intensity, coming like that out of the blue, and she began to shake, her fingers trembling in her lap. Of course he wouldn't come. How could he, when he knew nothing of what was going on? Matthew specialised in the condition, he knew all about the problems people had to cope with—that was why she had thought of him. That must be it. She'd seen the way he was with his patients, the way he coaxed them into looking on the bright side. His strength was inherent, a vital part of him; she could have leaned on him.

She sighed. What was she thinking of, wishing that he could be here with her? She was overwrought, and not being at all logical. She stared at her sister's still form. She felt so alone but there were people she ought to be contacting—her grandparents, and Rebeccah, her aunt. They would want to know what was going on, but she felt a strange reluctance to relay only bad news. It was still the middle of the night; they would be sleeping, tucked up safely in their beds, and there was no point in worrying them now. She'd tell them when she had something positive to say.

Gradually, she sensed a change in Sophie. Small signs, but distinct. And when the nurse came in she noticed it too. 'She's sleeping naturally, she's on the mend,' she said, and Becky let out a sigh, a long, shaky breath, as though she'd been holding it in for all this time.

A while later, Sophie woke briefly, and seemed a little confused. Becky returned her smile.

'Back to sleep,' she told her quietly. 'You're safe.' She touched her sister's cheek and gently brushed back the hair that had fallen over her temples, until Sophie closed her eyes and slept once more.

By breakfast-time, Sophie was propped up in bed and was allowed a drink.

'You scared me half to death,' Becky scolded quietly. 'Please don't ever do that to me again.'

Sophie leaned back against the pillows. There was more colour in her face now and Becky smiled at her, relief coursing through her veins.

'I'm not sure what happened,' Sophie murmured sleepily. 'I remember going to the disco. . .we met some boys there, they were chatting us up. Then on the way home I didn't feel so good. How long have I been here?'

'All night. Stacey's parents called an ambulance when you passed out.'

Sophie chewed at her lip. 'Have you been here all night?'

Becky nodded. 'I came as soon as I heard. I was so worried about you. The nurse thinks you must have missed out on your insulin injections—did you forget to do them?'

Sophie looked uncomfortable. 'I didn't think it would matter if I just missed one or two. . . I'd been feeling all right, and I didn't see why I couldn't just be like everyone else. No one else has to put up with injections and tests and diets. It doesn't seem fair.'

'I know it doesn't, but you aren't alone, Sophie. Lots of young people have diabetes, and they learn to adjust to it eventually, so that it doesn't interfere with their enjoyment of life.'

'I suppose you're going to suggest I join a contact group again, aren't you?' Sophie hunched her shoulders in a belligerent attitude. 'I already have plenty of friends, at school.'

'I wasn't about to suggest anything,' Becky said, recognising a familiar no-win situation, 'except that you try to get some rest. I'll see if I can find you some magazines, and then I'm going to ring the grandparents and Aunt Rebeccah. I'm sure they'll want to come and see you. Do you feel up to it?'

Sophie nodded. 'Aren't you supposed to be at work this morning? It's Saturday, isn't it? I thought it was your turn on the rota. You said. . .' She paused, thinking hard. 'You said you were going to be on duty this weekend with Dr Kingston. Matthew—that's his first name, isn't it? You weren't too sure about working with him when he first arrived, were you?'

'I'm getting used to him,' Becky answered. 'Yes, I was supposed to go in later this morning, but I could phone and get someone to stand in for me.'

Sophie shook her head. 'No, don't do that; it's only a couple of hours, isn't it? I wouldn't want you to get into trouble with him because of me.' She paused again. 'Mind you, you look all in; you'd probably do better to go home and get some sleep.'

'Look who's talking,' Becky retorted. 'You don't look so hot yourself.'

Sophie gave a faint smile. 'I *am* still tired,' she yawned.

'Then try to get some rest while I go and make some phone calls,' Becky said.

She phoned Aunt Rebeccah first, knowing that she could rely on her to organise the grandparents. They'd take it in turns to visit, providing the nursing staff said it would be all right.

Aunt Rebeccah arrived within the hour, bossy as ever. 'You go home and get some sleep,' she instructed Becky. 'You can come back later this afternoon.'

'OK,' Becky agreed. 'I'll bring a change of clothes with me, for Sophie.'

She didn't plan on staying at home, though. By the time she left the hospital it was getting on for the hour when she was due to put in an appearance at the surgery, and by then she'd left it far too late to arrange for anyone to take her place.

Some half an hour later, she walked wearily into

Reception at the health centre and checked her schedule for the morning. Suppressing a yawn, she scanned her list of patients. While she was doing that, Matthew came in to look at his own list, looking so unbelievably fit and energetic that she almost winced. Experimentally, she moved her tired shoulders, dropping the paper she was holding, and stooped to retrieve it.

He studied her, his mouth taking on a grim line. 'That much of a night, was it? You look as though you haven't slept at all. Doesn't your boyfriend realise you have work to do?'

'Since I'm perfectly able to do my job, I hardly think that's any of your business,' she retorted sharply, straightening. She saw the tightening line of his jaw and regretted her words as soon as she'd said them, but she wasn't up to explanations, and the last thing she needed was for him to start taking her to task, nor did she feel like being watched like a hawk for the rest of the day. He was doing it now, his glance moving over her features, and no doubt he was drawing his own conclusions about her paleness, her lacklustre eyes and the weary droop of her shoulders.

She drew herself up. 'If you're going to keep staring at me like that,' she said tartly, 'you're very soon going to get on my nerves.'

'I shouldn't have thought it would take much to do that this morning.' He walked away from her then, and she heard him go over to the corner of the room where the coffee-pot was steaming gently. There was a clatter of crockery, and a minute or so later he came back to her, pushing a cup towards her. 'Here. You'd better drink that. It'll at least pep you up a bit and put some colour in your cheeks.' It was a command, and the cool arrogance of his tone was enough to bait her.

'Thanks. Though, I'm quite capable of deciding for myself what I need.'

'Are you?' His eyes glittered as he ran his glance over

her stiffening figure, and she averted her gaze, sipping at the hot liquid and making an effort to sift through the papers on the desk.

She was aware of him, nevertheless, conscious of his scrutiny the whole time, and it goaded her into asking, 'Was there something you wanted? I'm not about to make any mistakes, if that's what you're thinking.'

'That wasn't what I was thinking, as a matter of fact,' he said smoothly, his mouth twisting. 'You're far too jumpy for your own good. I was simply going to ask whether we've received the report from the eye clinic yet, on Mr Harvey. I suspect it will show a degree of retinopathy.'

The easy glide from personal to business matters threw her precariously off balance. Chastened, she looked through the reports that had come in that morning. 'Yes,' she said, pulling a sheet from the pile. 'This must be the one. Early stages, from the looks of things, but there's certainly some damage to the blood vessels at the back of the eye. He'll need laser treatment, won't he?'

Matthew nodded, checking the report. 'It looks that way, but at least we have his diabetes control stabilised now. There shouldn't be any further deterioration.' He glanced through the contents of the folder a moment longer, and Becky gave a yawn. Immediately, his glance swivelled back to her. 'Am I keeping you up?' he enquired on a silky note.

Her mouth tightened, but before she could think of a suitably crushing reply the receptionist came over and said, 'Becky, your patient with the scalded wrist wants to know if you'll take a look at the dressing. She's early, but she has an appointment somewhere else in an hour.'

'Of course. I'll be right there.'

Matthew had turned away and was heading towards his own room. He'd obviously formed the wrong conclusion about the way she'd spent the night, and maybe she ought to have explained instead of jumping down his throat, but it was too late; there wasn't time now to stop and bandy words with him. Her waiting room was filling up fast, and she had better get a move on. In any case, she thought crossly, why should she feel she needed to explain anything to him? He didn't have to think the worst of her all the time, did he?

She was kept busier than usual for the next couple of hours. There had been a spate of accidents this morning, and Matthew was sending people through to her with marked regularity for dressings of various sorts.

Her last patient of the morning was an elderly man whose hand was gashed in several places, the skin red and angry looking.

'What have you been doing, Ben—pruning the roses?'

'That's right, love; I thought it was about time I cut them back. I seem to have been a bit careless today.'

'It'll need cleaning up,' she told him. 'Have you had a tetanus jab recently?'

He scratched his head. 'I did have one, some time. I can't really remember when it was, it could have been a few years back, I suppose.'

'Well, we'll give you another one just to be on the safe side,' she said. 'Next time, maybe you should think about wearing gloves.'

He sent her a rueful smile. 'That's what the wife said.'

When he'd gone, there was a gratifying peacefulness about the place and Becky quickly tidied up the clinic. She'd be glad to get home. Perhaps she'd have something to eat, then change her clothes and head back towards the hospital.

Satisfied at last that everything was in order, she put on her coat and walked out through the main door. Matthew glanced at her as she passed by him, but he was deep in conversation with the receptionist, and she went out of the building alone, feeling more desolate than ever. Perhaps it was just as well they didn't have the chance to talk, though. The mood she was in, she'd probably only

finish up antagonising him and flinging up even more
barriers than before. A heavy sigh escaped her, freezing
into a little cloud in the frosty air.

It was a miserable, bone-chilling morning and she
pulled up her coat collar as she walked along the path.
Some hot soup wouldn't go amiss and perhaps she'd call
in at the bakery and pick up a crusty loaf before she
went to her car.

She reached the street and stood at the bend of the
road for a moment, thinking about Sophie. She'd looked
so small and vulnerable this morning, just a confused
young girl, and somehow that brought back a tidal wave
of loneliness. Their whole family unit had been wrecked
over the last few years, and now there were just the two
of them, needing each other more than ever.

She'd checked the road, ready to cross, when there
was a sudden awful screeching of brakes, and in that
moment of confusion she could see a Range Rover swerv-
ing around the bend towards her. It was going to mount
the pavement, it was bound to hit her, she was directly
in its path, and there was no time to think, to take in the
full horror as it lunged towards her. She knew it couldn't
miss; she couldn't move quickly enough out of its way.
Thoughts dashed through her brain, and then her one
overriding concern was for Sophie, for Sophie being left
alone, and panic chilled her to the bone, spread icy fingers
through her veins.

Then, as the squeal of tyres dulled her brain, she felt
strong hands pulling her backwards, and she heard her
name being called. It seemed to come from a distance,
the sound echoing through mist—the mist of her bewil-
derment and shock. It swirled around her like a fog,
clouding her brain and freezing her into immobility. Her
breath had been held in terror at the inevitability of what
was about to happen, and now as the Range Rover hurtled
to a stop she found herself being pulled sideways out of
its path. She was held in strong arms, her face buried in

a man's jacket, a hand smoothing the hair at her nape.

'Becky, what the hell are you doing? What were you thinking of?'

The sharp tone cut through her, and she gasped, her mouth trembling. 'I don't. . .I thought. . .'

'You weren't thinking at all, you little fool. God, do you realise you might have been killed?'

Matthew's voice penetrated the fog, and her shocked eyes slowly opened, focusing bleakly on the wall at the place where she had been standing just a moment ago and where the Range Rover was now slammed against it, slewed at a rakish angle and yet without a dent on it.

'It was an accident. . . It happened so suddenly—'

The bull bars on the front were rammed up against the bricks, and it was the sight of the bars that broke her control. She thought of her father, and how he'd died, and sobs racked her chest.

Matthew's hold on her tightened, his fingers tangling in the hair at her nape. 'Let it out,' he said. 'Let it all out. You've had a nasty shock, but it's over now, I've got you. You're safe, Becky; you're safe.'

Tears stung her eyes and escaped down her cheeks, dampening his shirt-front. She was breathing hard, she felt weak and dizzy. He offered her a comforting shoulder, and she needed that right now. After a while, though, she dashed her fingers across her face and tried to straighten up. She saw the white-faced driver climb out of the car and come towards her, and she stared at him, feeling sick and bone-achingly cold.

'Are you all right?' he asked. 'I just didn't see you, until it was too late. There was a dog—it ran across the road in front of me, and I swerved to avoid it. I came round the bend and you were there. God, I almost hit you.'

She pressed her hands into her coat. 'I'm OK,' she said shakily. 'Are you hurt at all?'

He shook his head. 'No, I'm all right; luckily the seat

belt kept me from going through the windscreen. I don't think there's even a scratch on the car.'

She looked over at the Range Rover once more, and felt nausea rise in her throat. 'Why do you have those bars on your vehicle?' she said, her voice strained. 'Don't you know how dangerous they are, the dreadful injuries they cause? They ought to be banned. Have you thought what would have happened if a child had been there in my place? A child would have no chance, not with those things on the front; even grown men can be terribly hurt by them.'

The man stared at her blankly as though he didn't understand her outburst. 'They're just bull bars,' he said, his tone bewildered.

His puzzlement sent shards of ice through her veins. 'People die in accidents because of them,' she said tightly, her voice rising with agitation. 'You should get rid of them.'

She was shivering now, and if Matthew hadn't been holding her she would have surely fallen, her limbs were so weak.

'She's badly shocked,' he said to the driver. 'I'm going to take her home. What about you—are you going to be able to drive? Do you need help getting the vehicle back on the road?'

'I'm fine, really. Just a bit shaken up, that's all. That dog should have been on a lead, not allowed to roam free like that. It doesn't bear thinking about, what might have happened.'

Matthew nodded grimly, waiting while the man climbed into the driving seat and carefully straightened up the Range Rover and edged it back onto the road. Then, slowly, he led her away towards the health centre and the car park.

'Come on, let's get you home,' he muttered, his deep voice smoothing over her badly frayed nerves, and within minutes she was in his car, a blanket wrapped around her.

She remembered very little of the drive, but eventually they arrived at her house, and Matthew searched her bag for her keys, then let them both in through the front door. She stared at the empty hall, wondering what she was doing here.

'My car,' she said bleakly. 'I've left my car.'

'Forget it,' he said tersely.

She looked around but her vision was blurred, and she didn't have any real idea what to do next. She heard the front door being closed, and then Matthew was leading her towards the sitting room.

'Sit down,' he said, and he must have brought the blanket with him because she was wrapped up in it once again, and she realised that he'd taken time to light the fire. Then he took her in his arms and held her close against him, soothing her as though she were a baby.

'My car,' she said again, as though her mind was stuck in one revolution, as though it was the only solid thing she could focus on.

'I said forget it,' he repeated firmly. 'You don't have to worry about that. We'll organise something. You're in no state to drive right now.'

She struggled restlessly against his restraining hold. 'But I have to go—'

'You're going nowhere,' he said bluntly. 'You've had a bad shock, and you're not yourself. You haven't been yourself all morning.'

She looked up at him then, and saw the concern in his eyes. 'You saved me,' she said, remembering. 'You pulled me out of the way and I haven't even thanked you.'

'I'm just glad I was there in time,' he breathed. 'I could see what was going to happen, and I had to do something quickly.' His voice sounded rough around the edges. 'I don't think I've ever moved so fast in my life.'

He produced a clean handkerchief from his jacket pocket and gently wiped her face, drying away the tears that had trickled slowly down her cheeks. Damp strands of hair had fallen across her face and he gently pushed them back now, tucking them behind her ears. 'You were staring at the bull bars,' he said. 'Can you tell me about it? It wasn't just what happened today that upset you, was it? There's something more, isn't there? Can you tell me about it, Becky?'

A shudder coursed through her body as she remembered. 'My father died two years ago,' she told him. 'He was a TV engineer and it was just an ordinary day for him. He was on his way home after work, and he'd just stopped off at one of the shops. It was a Friday night, it was about this time of year, and it was dark already, and raining hard. There were trees lining the avenue and my father had gone to stand under one while he talked to a friend. They were sheltering there for a moment.'

Her fingers twisted in her lap. 'My father was going to go back to his car. He was coming home to us. He told his friend he'd bought fireworks for bonfire night; we were going to have a party, invite the neighbours and their children. Only. . .he never made it.' Her voice broke, and Matthew's arm tightened around her.

'Can you go on?'

She sniffed, then nodded. 'Some youths came around the corner. . .they were joyriders, and they were in a Range Rover, like the one we saw today, and they were going too fast, much too fast. They lost control and my father was knocked down and crushed against the tree. The man who was with him, his friend, was injured badly, but he lived.' She rubbed the back of her hand against her eyes. 'They couldn't save my father, though. The doctor said that if there hadn't been bull bars on the front of the vehicle his injuries might not have been so severe, but, as things were, he had no chance. . .'

She stared ahead, seeing nothing of her surroundings, only the stark images in her mind. 'When I saw that car coming towards me today, all I could think of was my father, and then Sophie, being left alone. It was as though I was frozen, I didn't seem to be able to move.'

'It must have been terrible for you,' Matthew said, his head bending so that his cheek brushed hers. 'I'm so sorry, Becky, so very sorry.' His palm flattened on her spine, drawing her to him, and she buried her face once more in his jacket.

'You've had a bad day, haven't you, sweetheart? But it's over now. Try to forget what happened, put it behind you.' He kissed her then, tenderly on the forehead, and she closed her eyes, absorbing his warmth and his gentleness. She'd forgotten what it was like to have someone look after her, to care about her in such a selfless way, and the temptation to give in to it and let him comfort her was almost overwhelming.

But she mustn't get used to this, he was just being sympathetic, that was all. She'd had to stand on her own two feet these last few years and that was how it would always be. She had to pull herself together. Drawing back from him a little, she tried to compose herself. Matthew was looking at her, and she could see that he was concerned.

'You feel so cold,' he murmured, touching her cheek lightly with his fingers. 'I'll make you some tea, and something hot to eat. You'll feel better with something warm inside you.'

He eased away from her, but she could see that he wasn't sure about leaving her and so she tried to smile and sat up a little straighter and said, 'I'll be all right now, I promise. Thanks, Matthew.'

He went into the kitchen, and came back after a few minutes with tea and soup and said, 'I managed to find my way about your kitchen. I thought soup would warm you, and it was quick and easy.'

He came and sat beside her. They didn't talk much as they ate. There didn't seem to be any need for words, and it was enough that he was there, strong and warm and dependable.

After a while, though, other thoughts came crowding back, she remembered other things about the day, and said quietly, 'I need to get my car. Would you take me back to the centre to fetch it?'

'You've been worrying about that ever since we came here, but we can do it later, can't we? What's the rush?'

'I should be at the hospital with Sophie,' she began, and then she told him what had happened last night. 'I just have to get a few things together for her.'

He frowned, staring down at her, his eyes darkening with something akin to anger. 'Why on earth didn't you say something this morning? You shouldn't even have been at work.'

Becky shrugged, pulling the blanket from her shoulders. 'Perhaps I needed to be with people,' she muttered. 'And it wasn't as though I had to put in a full day at the centre.'

His mouth tightened. 'You didn't think of telling me, of letting me know what you'd been through, did you?' He studied her, a muscle flicking in his jaw. 'I can hardly believe you could be so breathtakingly, stubbornly independent.'

'I would have, I think. . .but. . .' Her voice trailed away and he stared at her in exasperation.

'I'll drive you to the hospital,' he said tersely, and when she would have argued the grim set of his mouth made her subside. 'We'll see about picking up your car on the way back, but if you're not up to it we'll fetch it tomorrow.'

Becky let the blanket drop behind her on the settee as she stood up. 'I'll go upstairs and get a few things together. I won't be more than a few minutes.'

He got to his feet with her, and she left him pacing the carpet, his glance skimming the room. She'd done what she could to give the place a homely, lived in look, with bright cushions on the sofa and carefully chosen pictures on the walls, and she wondered what he thought of her efforts.

When she came downstairs a short time later, he was leafing through Sophie's sketch-book, which had been lying on the table. There were one or two portraits in there, of herself and Rebeccah, and one of Drew, but the pictures were mostly landscapes—places they'd visited or that had special meaning for Sophie.

He was frowning and she said hesitantly, 'There's really no need for you to come with me, all the way to the hospital. I feel fine now; I can manage if you want to go.'

'I said I'd take you,' he reminded her curtly, and she bit her lip, wondering what she'd said or done to make him react in such a fierce manner. Perhaps he was simply regretting his earlier generosity of spirit, and now he felt unable to ease himself out of the situation. There was no time to dwell on that, though, because he closed the sketch-book abruptly and said, 'If you're ready, we'd better go.'

CHAPTER FIVE

THIS time, as she sat beside him on the drive to the hospital, Becky was able to absorb the sheer comfort of simply relaxing in the luxurious interior of Matthew's car. She leaned back into the cushioning upholstery, watching his capable hands on the wheel, her senses lulled by the quiet hum of the engine, and she was hardly conscious of her eyelids growing gradually heavier. His shoulder was close, his arm warmly brushing her own. It was a comforting feeling, having him so near.

It was only later, when she heard his quiet voice, that she realised the car was no longer moving. She blinked, coming awake slowly, and looked up into a pair of glittering green eyes. Her head had slipped sideways, cradled comfortably against his shoulder, and the warm male scent of him invaded her nostrils.

'I'm sorry,' she murmured self-consciously. 'I didn't mean to fall asleep like that. What must you think of me?'

His sensuous mouth tilted. 'I think you're obviously exhausted, and once you've seen your sister the best thing you could do would be to go home and get straight into bed. With me for company, preferably, but that's probably the last thing you need right now.'

His words took her breath away, and hot colour flooded her cheeks as her imagination took hold and she saw herself locked in his arms.

'Matthew, I—'

'Hell—' He cut off her words with a mind-shattering, bruising kiss that left her pulse racing out of control and her body trembling with need. It was just as well she was sitting down, because there was no substance to her limbs; she was totally absorbed in the feel of his mouth on hers, and her own desperate urgency to respond.

Then the sound of a car starting up in the distance filtered through to her dazed brain. Her fingers twisted in his shirt and she groaned restlessly, remembering where they were. Matthew must have realised too, because he reluctantly eased himself away from her and said thickly, 'My timing's way off, isn't it? Things are confused enough, and this isn't exactly the place. . .I didn't bring you here for this.'

Disorientated, she rubbed her eyes and sat up stiffly in her seat, peering through the window. They were in the car park and the main buildings of the hospital loomed just a few yards away. She swallowed, coming slowly back to stark reality, and he pushed open the door and began to climb out of the car.

He gave her a wry smile as she joined him on the tarmac. 'Let's go.'

'I don't know how I'd have coped without you today,' she murmured, finding her voice. 'I seem to be forever in your debt.'

'I'm glad to help,' he told her dismissively. 'I just wish that you'd said something before and not tried to struggle with everything alone. You've had a lot to cope with just lately, haven't you? It couldn't have been easy, moving house, seeing to all the arrangements as well as keeping an eye on your sister. Have you settled into the place all right? Are things any easier now that you're closer to the centre?'

She sensed he was talking to calm things down, to bring them back on course. Maybe he was regretting what had happened. Her response had been immediate, soaring, but—coming back down to earth—neither of them had been looking for involvement. It was just the events of the day that had taken over and clouded things.

She nodded. 'It'll be much better in the winter. Where we used to live, the country roads could be very tricky once the snow came—but I couldn't have stayed there, anyway. There were too many memories for both of us.'

'You said you were renting Sarah's house—haven't you thought about buying a place of your own?' He retrieved the overnight bag from the boot of the car and they walked over to the hospital.

'I have thought about it,' Becky answered, 'but I wanted to put some money in trust for Sophie after I sold the house, and I need more time to think about the future. Besides, Sarah's house is convenient for both of us; the rent isn't very high, and I think we'd do well to stay there. I don't want to uproot Sophie again.'

They went into the main building and took the lift to the ward. A table and some comfortable armchairs were set out in a waiting area off the corridor, and Matthew said, 'I'll wait here for you. You'll want to see your sister alone for a while.'

'You can't stay out here,' she started to object. 'You must come with me.' But he was already picking up a newspaper from the table.

'I mean it. You go on in.' He had that look about his mouth again, and she knew it would be a waste of time to argue with him.

'I'll tell her that you're here,' she said, compromising. 'Then you can come and join us.'

Aunt Rebeccah was sitting at the side of the bed, and as Becky walked in she came over to her and gave her a hug.

'You're almost as pale as your sister,' she chided. 'What have the pair of you been up to? I can see I shall have to take you both in hand. I was just asking Sophie if she'd like to spend next week with me; your uncle John won't be needing me at the factory—they're not all that busy this month—and I know he'd love to have her stay—you too, Becky.'

'I'd love to come for a day or so,' Becky answered, 'but I have to work next week and it will be easier for me if I'm at the house. Of course Sophie can stay longer, if she'd like.'

She turned to look at her sister. 'How are you feeling now, love?'

'A lot better than I did last night and this morning,' Sophie said with a grin. 'But you don't look so good. I don't know how you managed to drive here, even.'

'I didn't. Dr Kingston brought me.'

'I knew it—you've been in to work, haven't you? Where is he?' demanded their aunt.

Becky pulled a face. 'He insisted on staying outside in the corridor.'

'Outside?' Aunt Rebeccah's eyes widened. 'We can't have that—tell him to come in. I'm going to get myself a cup of tea anyway, so you can chat without the nurses coming in to tell you off.'

Becky's glance went to Sophie. 'Do you feel up to more visitors?' She didn't like the idea of Matthew waiting out there either, though she wondered whether he was just distancing himself from her, not wanting to get involved any more than he already was. The thought made her feel strangely lonely.

Sophie shrugged. 'I feel OK,' she said.

Becky went to fetch Matthew. 'You don't have any choice,' she told him. 'You're under orders to come and meet my family.'

He grinned at her. 'Well, if you're going to put it like that. . .'

He went back to the ward with her, and looked at Sophie, his expression wry. 'What on earth have you been up to, young lady, to land yourself in here? It wasn't Becky's cooking that did it, was it?'

Sophie spluttered with laughter, while Becky poked him in the ribs, bristling with good-humoured indignation. 'Of all the cheek!'

Sophie sobered and studied him in return with solemn grey eyes. 'You're the new doctor at the centre, aren't you?' she asked.

Matthew nodded. 'That's right.'

'Becky said you work with diabetic patients. But you'll be moving on, you're not staying around there for long.'

'I'm just filling in until after Christmas,' Matthew told her. 'Then I'm going to work at a practice where there's a large clinic attached. I'll be seeing a lot more diabetic patients than I do at the moment.' He paused. 'So, do you know how you came to end up here?'

Sophie made a face. 'Everyone makes such a fuss, but it's no big deal.'

Becky chewed at her lip but stayed silent, and Matthew said, 'Well, I'm sure they're taking good care of you, anyway. Have the doctors talked to you about the reasons for your collapse?'

'They said it was to do with not taking the insulin.' She yawned, then added, 'They say I might be able to go home today.' She looked at Becky. 'Is it all right if we go and stay with Aunt Rebeccah?'

'Of course.'

Sophie yawned again and Matthew said, 'Perhaps you should get some sleep and build your strength up again for when you come home. Will you get the chance to do some sketching when you're at your aunt's house? I saw some of the drawings you've done. You're very talented. . .it must be something you enjoy doing.'

'I do it when I feel like it. It depends whether I see something I want to sketch. Mostly I draw or paint things that interest me. People or places that are important to me.'

'I'll have to pack you some more things for next week anyway,' Becky said. 'I could always put one of your sketch-books in with them. There are some good land-scapes around Aunt Rebeccah's house.'

They talked for a while longer, until Sophie grew sleepy and eventually dozed off. Becky went and found the nursing staff and spoke to them, making arrangements for later on that day.

'You might as well go home and get some rest,' the

nurse told her. 'The doctor will want to see her this evening, but if he gives the all clear then she can go home.'

Rebeccah echoed the advice. 'I'll stay around here,' she said, 'and you can phone up later. You look all in— do as you're told and go on home.'

Becky was quiet as she and Matthew walked back to the car some time later, and he must have picked up on her unconscious vibes, because he asked quietly, 'What's wrong?'

'I feel as though I should be staying,' Becky admitted. 'None of this should have happened. It's all my fault, I should have watched her more carefully. I feel as though I've neglected her terribly.'

'You know that isn't true,' Matthew said shortly. 'You've made a home for her, you've taken the place of both her parents. You must know that youngsters go through stages like this. Sophie's probably like any other teenager—she feels rebellious and resentful at times. She wants to be like everyone else in her group of friends, and who can blame her for that? None of this is your fault. You're too close to the situation, that's all, and you're not looking at it in an objective way. You don't have to feel that it's any slight on you because your aunt wants to take care of her.'

Becky coloured a little at that. Matthew was too perceptive by far. She said, 'It's just that I feel so guilty. My aunt's been very good to both of us, over the years. She stepped in when my mother died, and she was there for us after my dad's accident. I know she means well and there's no reason for me to feel like this.'

'You're chastising yourself because you're over-tired and overwrought,' Matthew said firmly. 'What you need is a break. You need to get away from the responsibility for a while, to do something completely different. Perhaps if you can stand back from the situation you'll see

things more clearly and see that you've nothing to blame
yourself for.'

They reached the car and he opened the passenger
door for her. As she slid into the seat, he rested his hands
against the car roof and looked down at her. 'There's
another ramble set up for next weekend. Why don't you
join me? It'll do you good to get out in the fresh air,
forget your worries for a while.'

Becky turned his suggestion over in her mind. Perhaps
he was right, she could do with a change.

'Maybe I will, at that,' she agreed, 'if Sophie's back to
normal by then,' and his mouth curved with satisfaction.

'That's my girl,' he said, walking around to his side
of the car. 'The change will do you good.'

He took her home, and insisted on walking back to
the centre to fetch her car. She wondered whether he
might come in when he returned, and she spent the next
half-hour in a state of nervous excitement tinged with a
measure of uncertainty.

'You look all in,' he said with a dry smile as he handed
her the keys, and she was about to deny it, except that
a huge yawn took her off guard, and he grinned. 'Off to
bed,' he ordered. 'Try to get some sleep. I'm very
tempted to stay, but I have to go and call in on a patient.'

Perhaps that was just as well, she reasoned some time
later when she had her thoughts more in order. It had
been a traumatic day, one way and another, and she
needed time to get things into perspective. Throughout
the course of the following week, she had misgivings
about her decision to go with him on the ramble, but
Sophie was feeling fine, and Matthew had already told
some of the others at the centre that he'd persuaded her
to give it a try; she didn't think she could go back on
their agreement without having to give a deal of explanation. They would read more into it than there was and
she didn't want to risk that.

It had come home to her that getting involved with

Matthew outside the practice was a tricky enough situation to handle, without having to cope with wagging tongues as well. She ought never to have gone against her better judgement, mixing her work with her private life, and she hadn't sorted out her relationship with Drew yet. Not properly, finally. He'd phoned the centre and left a message for her to call him, and she at least owed it to him to talk things through.

It was too late to back down with Matthew, though. He'd caught her at a low moment, and the deed was done. He was holding her to it. She'd even tried telling him that she didn't think she had the right gear for a ramble, but he'd scotched that objection straight away.

'I should be able to fix you up with what you need,' he said. 'Walking boots, waterproofs, and a rucksack, in case you want to take a flask and a bite to eat. I know someone who'll probably help out, and if she can't provide everything someone at the club will be able to help out. We like to encourage new people to give it a try.'

It was as though he'd known she was trying to find some way out and he was blocking her every attempt. In the end, she decided to give in gracefully, and agreed to have him pick her up from her aunt's house on Saturday.

Uncle John opened the door to him while Becky was still getting ready. She applied a last coat of lipstick and dabbed it with a tissue as she heard her uncle showing Matthew into the living room.

'She won't be long,' John said cheerfully. 'You know what these women are, fussing about with their hair and make up and so on. She'll be down in a minute.'

Becky wished he hadn't said that. It made it sound as though she was going to a lot of trouble, and she didn't want Matthew thinking that, even though she had spent the morning in a state of unaccountable nervousness. It wasn't a date, after all, just an afternoon out, a chance to grab some fresh air and enjoy the countryside.

Sophie came out of the kitchen as Becky walked down the stairs into the hall. 'Does this mean Drew's off the scene?' she wanted to know. 'Have you had a row or something?'

'No, nothing like that,' Becky told her uneasily, because they hadn't actually fallen out as such, had they? Drew wanted to go on as before. In his mind, it had just been a disagreement, something that needed to be sorted out between them. It was Becky who had the problem of what to do.

Sophie's mouth made a little grimace. 'So where is he this weekend?'

Becky wondered about that grimace. She sensed that Sophie had never really taken to Drew, but she hadn't ever come right out and said anything. Now she said, 'He phoned me a few days ago to say he had to go away—something to do with extending his premises. There are people he needs to talk to.'

Their conversation was cut short just then as Aunt Rebeccah came into the hall. 'Ah, there you are, Sophie. Your uncle John's about ready to take us to the cinema.'

'OK. I'll go and get my coat.'

Becky watched Sophie walk away, then turned and saw that Matthew was standing by the door, one hand resting against the jamb.

'Perhaps we should be going too,' he said. His expression was cool as he looked her over, a diamond spark in his eyes, and she hoped there wasn't anything wrong with the way she had dressed. True to his word, he'd found her the things she needed for the day, though she was wearing her own jeans and a sweater under a warm jacket, and she'd tucked the waterproofs he'd given her into the rucksack on the hall table. 'Do the boots fit?' he asked. 'I thought Rachel was about your size.'

'They're just perfect,' she said. She felt an unwilling curiosity about this woman who had lent them, and a small knot of tension coiled in her stomach. 'She must be a good friend, to lend out these things.'

'Yes, she is.' His mouth made an odd shape. 'I've known her for a long time. Years, in fact.'

Becky absorbed the information soberly. If he'd known her that length of time. . . She couldn't pursue the thought. Instead, she asked, 'Does she do a lot of walking?'

'Not so much nowadays. She used to belong to the club. . .' He hesitated a moment, and Becky thought she saw a fleeting expression of sadness touch his features, but it was gone so quickly that she might have imagined it. 'We used to pair up on the walks. It's a bit more difficult for her now that she has the children,' he went on. 'They have their own interests, and I suppose she likes to encourage them. They do a lot of things together at the weekend.'

He finished on a preoccupied note, and she shot him a quick glance, but he was giving nothing away. Perhaps that was just as well. The more she heard, the more tense she became. The way he spoke about her, the tone he used, made her wonder if there had been something between them. It was just a thought, an impression, but. . .

Rachel had children, so clearly she was married. Had that been the reason behind his preoccupation? Oh, she was tying herself in knots just wondering. . .needing to know, yet not wanting to know.

'Do you see much of her? I'll have to return these things,' she added hastily.

'I'll do it. I've had to go over to her place quite often lately. She's on her own a lot just now, and she needs someone to talk to. Things haven't been easy for her, and she needs a shoulder to lean on—' He broke off. 'It's time we were on our way.'

They said their goodbyes a few minutes later and drove to the meeting point on a village green ten miles away. About a dozen people were assembled there, with maps and rucksacks, kitted out in much the same fashion as

she and Matthew. They were a cheerful crowd, with a
wide age range, and when Matthew introduced her
around she felt that there were people here that she could
make friends with, people who shared a sense of humour
and a feeling of well-being. Her thoughts about the day
were beginning to brighten.

'Have a hot drink before we start out,' a woman
offered, pouring coffee from a flask into a plastic cup,
while Matthew went to check out the route with someone
across the green.

'You're well kitted out, anyway,' one of the group
commented—a man, in his late sixties, she judged, from
his thinning grey hair and weather-beaten features. 'It's
a good idea to have strong walking boots—you don't
feel the bumps underfoot nearly so much.'

'They're borrowed from one of Matthew's friends. . .
Rachel,' she confessed. 'But if I decide to take up rambling on a regular basis I suppose I ought to buy some.'

'You'll enjoy it, I'm sure. Rachel used to come along
every month after Matthew introduced her. Mind you,
she was sweet on him at the time, so perhaps that's why
she was so keen. There was even talk of wedding bells,
till she met his best friend. Surprised everyone when she
married him instead. Matthew never seemed to want to
get involved with anyone else after that. Not properly,
anyway. Concentrated on his career instead—' He broke
off then, with a slight cough as his wife poked him in
the ribs. Becky tried not to show her dismay.

'The girl doesn't want to hear about that, Sean, now,
does she?' the woman said. 'It's all past and gone.'

'She still comes with us, doesn't she? Not as often, I
grant you, but she has other things to do with her weekends now, I expect.' Sean had obviously missed his
wife's point, but he didn't go on in the same vein, and
Becky didn't know whether she was glad of that or frus-
trated by knowing just a snippet. On the whole, she
supposed unhappily, it depended on how Matthew felt

about the situation, and that was something he was keeping to himself.

Ten minutes later they set off along the village street, walking on until they came to a green track that disappeared between houses and led towards an area of green fields. There had been a hard frost the night before and for most of the morning the ground had been crystalline, crisp underfoot and glittering with diamond lights. Now, though, the sun was out, high in the sky, and the frost was gradually melting away.

'It's a circular walk,' Matthew told her, 'and not a particularly long one, so we should be finished well before it gets dark. Have you been along these tracks before?'

'No, I'm almost ashamed to say that I haven't.' She shook her head, causing the bright chestnut curls to dance lightly in the breeze, and Matthew's glance followed the action.

She climbed a stile after him and Matthew helped her down from it, keeping his arm around her as they trudged over the uneven ground. It was warm and supportive and she felt a tingling, burning awareness ripple through her body at his touch. She was glad of his nearness, but her thoughts were tinged with uncertainty.

Did he still care deeply for Rachel? What was their relationship now? There was no time to dwell on it, though. The rough terrain demanded all her attention. There were hoof prints along the ground, embedded deep and as the frost melted they were beginning to turn to mud. As Sean had implied she would be earlier, Becky was glad of the sturdy walking boots. They made the going easier.

They crossed fields where hedgerows were bright with berries, then followed the passage of a brook that rippled noisily over stones. At one point a footbridge crossed it and Matthew led the way over this, following a track that took them uphill towards a quiet country road.

Becky's mouth curved at the sight which met her at the end of the road. 'Matthew, it's lovely,' she said, her voice rising in delight, her gaze following the line of a small lake, where ducks swam under a stone bridge towards a reedy island. A stone built house edged her view to the left, and to the right was what must have been the village hall. A banner advertised a craft fair, and people were moving in and out of the open doorway, some heading towards a little teashop. It was fronted by an overgrown shrubbery and tall trees.

He smiled down at her, an arm tugging her close. 'I thought you'd like it. In the summer it's beautiful, but even on a day like this it has a picture-postcard quality.' His eyes traced the smile which lit her features. 'This outing must be doing you some good,' he murmured. 'There's colour in your cheeks now and you look as though you've been enjoying yourself.'

'I have,' she laughed. 'I wasn't quite sure what to expect. I didn't know whether we'd be walking for the whole of the time, and I wasn't so sure whether I could stand up to so much exercise all in one go. It's been a long time since I walked such a distance.'

His green eyes glinted with amusement. 'You'll be safe enough with me,' he said. 'I wouldn't let you overdo things. Besides, there'd be hell to pay back at the centre if you were put out of action because of anything I'd persuaded you into. The place might fall apart without you.'

She made a face at that. 'That's highly unlikely with Martyn at the helm.'

They moved over to the bridge and stood for a while looking down at the water. Matthew's hand gently curved about her shoulder, keeping her close to him, his warm breath lightly fanning her cheek. The feel of his hard, strong body made her senses leap crazily, filled her with a powerful longing to be gathered into his arms and crushed against him, to taste his lips on hers. Almost as though he had read her thoughts, in the next instant his arms tightened around her, turning her and pressing her against his muscled length. Then his mouth came down on hers, demanding, exploring, until she clung to him, soft moans of pleasure lingering in her throat.

There was no thought in her head but this spiralling need to have more of him, to cling to him as though her life depended on it, and when he finally released her she almost swayed, her body clamouring with dizzying sensation, her legs incredibly weak.

'Someone's coming,' he said on a harsh breath, and she blinked, following the direction of his glance, her gaze fastening blankly on a man walking his dog. 'I expect the rest of the group will be along any minute. We'd better go.' He took her hand in his, turning away towards the path. 'Some are probably already in the hall, looking around the craft fair.'

She came slowly back to normal, taking in their surroundings once more. Her head was beginning to clear, and the moment had gone. *He* hadn't forgotten where they were, though, had he? He'd flirted with her, that was all—taken the opportunity as it had presented itself.

She swallowed hard. 'I think I'd like to look at it too,' she said as they started to walk. 'Would there be time, do you think? It would be a shame to miss the opportunity. I might be able to find something to cheer up Sophie, and perhaps a gift for Aunt Rebeccah. She's been good to us.'

'Of course, if that's what you want. We'll be stopping here for an hour or so.' His glance moved over her. 'They're never far from your thoughts, are they, your family, your responsibilities? Maybe you should try to forget them once in a while.'

He was echoing what Drew had said, but she pushed the errant thought from her mind. They went into the village hall and she took her time going round various stalls, conscious of Matthew by her side as she wandered from one to another. Most of the stalls were indoors, though some had been set out on a paved area at the back, a sheltered place made attractive by groups of shrubs and ornamental trees.

There was a lot to see—stalls with wickerwork and corn dollies and knick-knacks. She browsed at the jewellery stall for a while, examining delicate bracelets and pretty rings, but it was the table filled with handmade stuffed animals that delighted her most. There was a fluffy tiger cub just begging to be cuddled, and she picked it up, her mouth curving in a smile. 'I can't resist him.'

'Is he going to keep you warm in bed at night?' Matthew's voice rumbled deeply against her ear, and she looked up at him with laughter in her eyes.

'Why not?' she murmured. 'I'm sure I could find room for him. My bed's not exactly crowded.' She said it without thinking, then pulled in a breath.

'I'm glad.'

Her body responded to his words with a rush of heat that seemed to melt her bones. His gaze glittered over her, and he was so close that she could feel his warmth, and the subtle fragrance of his cologne teased her nostrils, tugging at her senses. She was fascinated by the clean angularity of his features, and she felt a sudden urge to run her fingers over the line of his jaw, to trace a path over the bronzed column of his throat.

Perhaps he'd read her mind, because his mouth twitched, his eyes teased. Just in time, she recovered her wits and remembered his will-o'-the-wisp nature, his constant need to move on. She was just a diversion for him, that was all. With a supreme effort of will-power, she resisted the urge, and reluctantly placed the tiger back on the table.

'Maybe I should show a little restraint, after all. There's the rest of the afternoon to go, and I'm loaded up as it is.'

He looked over her purchases. 'I shouldn't think there's much left on the stalls, is there?'

'You've been very patient,' she told him with a wry

smile as she pushed her purse back into the pocket of her jacket. 'My dad used to get bored stiff going on shopping trips. He said women were much better at that sort of thing, and he'd only be in the way, so he'd do us all a favour by staying home to watch the football on TV. We didn't mind—it meant he couldn't complain too much about the amount of money we'd spent, since he'd left us to it.' The memory brought with it an unexpected pang of loss, and she bent her head, concentrating on tucking the purchases she'd made into her bag.

If he noticed her sudden abstraction, Matthew tactfully made no comment. He said lightly, 'I have to help organise this kind of sale from time to time. I'm on the committee of a diabetes association, and we raise funds by holding this sort of event.' He glanced at the tie-dyed shirt she was folding into a corner of the rucksack. 'Is that for you?'

His mouth made an odd quirk, and she chuckled. 'You don't think it's quite me? I think the colours blend together rather beautifully. Something to relax in after a day's work—'

'You bought it for Sophie, didn't you?' He grinned, catching on. 'Yes, I imagine she'll love it. It will appeal to the artist in her.'

'That's what I thought. It has Sophie stamped all over it.'

'She has a definite talent for art,' Matthew commented as they left the hall. 'Is she planning on doing anything in that line when she leaves school?'

'She doesn't have anything in mind yet. I keep trying to persuade her to stay on. I think she could do an art course. But maybe I'm too close to her; she doesn't seem to listen.'

It was a problem she'd have to face head on, sooner or later. Sophie was bent on throwing away her chances, and all Becky's instincts told her that she had to do what she could to prevent her sister from wasting her opportunities. This wasn't the time or place to think over her problems, though, and she pushed them to one side and went with Matthew into the little teashop across the green.

Others in their group had the same idea, and they ate lunch companionably, chatting about this and that until it was time to set off once more. Feeling replete, they wandered out into the cool air.

'Where to now?' Becky asked.

'By the old mill and then on towards the woods,' Matthew told her. 'The ground gets pretty hilly over this way. Perhaps we should have eaten later.' He grinned at her and she sent him an answering smile.

'You could be right. I'll probably live to regret that apple pie yet.'

For the next hour or so they followed the other ramblers along winding tracks, over stiles and fences, until they reached a small wooded area that flanked the hillside.

'There's a path through the trees,' Matthew said, pointing out the way. 'Beyond that there's a small farm, and there's a footpath that we can follow through the fields.'

The sound of bird song filled the air as they walked into the woods. The trees were bare of leaves and stood stark against the skyline, and the ground was treacherous underfoot, so that they had to pick their way carefully through the twisted tree roots that spread out along the ground. It was cool here and Becky shivered a little, despite the warmth of her jacket. Almost instantly, Matthew's arm came around her, drawing her close.

'You're cold,' he murmured. 'Let me warm you.' Looking up at the sky, he added, 'It's clouding over. That means it will be getting dark early this afternoon.'

Becky nodded, finding it difficult to say anything at all when his arms folded around her and a heated current of electricity shot through her body. Just then, a shrill cry cut the air, and they broke away from each other in unison, turning towards the sound. It hadn't sounded like an animal. There had been a more human ring to it that filled Becky with alarm, and she looked up at Matthew, trying to gauge his response. She saw, from his frown, that he had had much the same reaction. 'That sounded as though someone's hurt,' she said.

'I think you could be right,' he agreed. 'Let's go and see what's happened.'

They stepped carefully over the rough ground, following a tricky path that was hidden in part by stones and stubbly undergrowth, until they came upon the group of ramblers ahead. Someone was lying on the ground and people were standing around, uncertain what to do.

'It's Madge, she's just had a nasty fall,' one of the men told Matthew, looking anxious. 'I should have been helping her but I turned away for a moment to talk to someone and she must have gone over one of those tree roots.'

'Let me take a look,' Matthew said, at once briskly efficient, going down on his knees to assess the extent of the damage. Becky went with him, crouching down beside the woman, whose face was white and contorted with pain. She remembered her from the morning— Sean's wife, a kindly retired bank clerk, who'd offered a flask of coffee when they'd first met.

Madge tried to move, then cried out again—a sharp agonised sound.

'Stay where you are, Madge; let me see what damage you've done.' Matthew examined her carefully, his expression thoughtful but filled with growing compassion. Becky could see from the way her foot was turned outwards and her leg seemed shortened that they were probably dealing with a hip fracture.

'It looks like a break, I'm afraid. We'll have to get you to hospital.' He stood up and took off his jacket, placing it gently over the woman's legs. It wouldn't be enough to warm her, Becky knew, and she quickly removed her own jacket, draping it carefully over the woman's shoulders. They had to prevent shock from setting in. It was going to be difficult enough to deal with the situation out here as it was, so far from the road.

'Just lie still,' Matthew said again, his voice calm and reassuring. 'We'll take care of everything.' It was doubtful whether Madge understood what he was saying, though, because she seemed confused, and beads of sweat had broken out on her face. In an undertone Matthew said to Becky, 'It looks like a fracture. I don't want to move her without proper equipment, but we're going to have to get her to hospital quickly.' He grimaced. 'It's unfortunate that I don't have my medical bag with me. I left it in the car.'

'Is there a short cut? You said this was a circular walk, so we can't be all that far from where you parked. I could go and get it for you while you stay with her.'

He nodded, thinking quickly. 'OK. There's a path which leads directly to the farm. You might be able to phone for an ambulance from there. Failing that, you can use the phone in my car. They'll have to bring a stretcher through on foot, but at least you'll be able to guide them to us. Take Madge's husband, Sean, with you—it'll be better for him to be occupied doing something useful, and he knows the way.'

Becky stood up, taking the keys he offered. 'I'll get back to you as soon as I can. She'll need something for the pain, poor soul.'

'She will. In the meantime, I'll do what I can for her here.' He was already turning back to his patient, but he added softly, 'Take care, Becky.'

'I will.'

Sean wanted to stay at first, but Matthew was right, he needed to keep busy, and after a few moments of discussion he set off with her along the path which would lead them to the farm.

Going as fast as they could, it was fifteen minutes
before they reached the farmhouse, but once there, Sean
was able to phone for an ambulance, and Becky left him
with the farmer's wife while she went on across the fields
in search of the green and Matthew's car. He had left it
in a leafy byway and she ran over to it, unlocked the
boot and took out the medical case. Sean was waiting
for her at the house when she returned.

'The ambulance is on its way,' he said, 'but it'll take
about another fifteen minutes to get here.'

'You stay, then, and direct them to us,' Becky told
him. 'I know my way back through the woods. I'll take
this case to Matthew.'

'Will you be all right on your own?' He glanced up
at the darkening sky.

'Of course,' Becky said. 'Don't worry.' She'd found
a torch in the boot of Matthew's car, together with a
blanket, and she'd brought them along with her, guessing
that they'd be needing them both. She shivered as she
went on her way, feeling the chill strike her bones as she
entered the woods. The air was damp with drizzle, and
the moisture was gradually seeping through her sweater,
adding to her discomfort. As she reached Matthew, she
saw that he was crouched on the ground beside Madge,
making her as comfortable as was possible in the circumstances.

'Well done,' he said as Becky knelt down beside him
and handed him the case. 'You made good time.
Where's Sean?'

'He's staying behind to direct the ambulance crew.
They shouldn't be too long now. How's she doing?'

'She's holding up,' he said in a quiet aside. 'We just
have to hope they can operate quickly once she gets
to hospital. There's always a better chance of complete
recovery if they can get to Theatre within
twenty-four hours.'

Becky watched him prepare an injection, then when

he had finished she spread the blanket over the woman's still form, tucking it gently around her.

'We'll soon have you warm and secure, Madge,' Matthew said. Turning to Becky, he added, 'I think we can send everyone else on their way, don't you? There's no point in them hanging around here waiting when it's getting darker all the time.'

Becky nodded. 'I'll go and talk to them,' she said.

When she came back and crouched beside him a few moments later, he asked, 'Was it difficult finding your way through the woods back here? It couldn't have been easy with darkness falling.'

'I had this torch,' she said. 'It wasn't too bad.' She didn't tell him how scared she'd felt, how eerie it had seemed coming through those woods. She glanced at Madge and hoped for her sake that the crew would get here quickly with the stretcher.

Becky shivered, feeling clammy now with cold, and Matthew put his arm around her. 'As soon as we have her safely on her way, we'll go back to my place; it's nearer than yours. We can warm up there and find a change of clothes.'

The paramedics arrived about a quarter of an hour later. Becky watched with relief as they carefully transferred Madge to a stretcher and then set off slowly through the woods back towards the waiting ambulance. Matthew and Becky went ahead, leaving Sean to walk alongside his wife. Matthew had the torch now and he used it to light up the way, picking out the rough ground.

When they reached the farm, they waited while Madge and Sean had transferred to the ambulance, watching as it moved away on the road to the hospital. The farmer, back from the fields by then, gave them a lift to the village green, dropping them off alongside Matthew's car. They'd retrieved their jackets but the cold had seeped into Becky, freezing her to the bone, so that she didn't think she'd ever feel warm again.

'I'll put the heater on; it should help,' Matthew said as they climbed into the car, and she sank into the passenger seat, wrapping her arms about her. 'You didn't have a very good introduction to rambling, did you?' he added on a rueful note as he drove along, the car's lights piercing the gloom ahead. 'I'm sorry it couldn't have been better for you.'

'No one can foresee this kind of thing happening,' Becky answered with a faint smile. 'And, to be honest, I had a wonderful time until Madge's accident. The air seemed so clean and fresh, it made me feel glad to be alive...to begin with, at least.' Another shiver racked her body.

Matthew glanced sideways at her. 'Not so good now, though; you look as though you've been packed in ice.'

'At least I was able to keep on the move, and that stopped me from freezing altogether,' Becky told him. 'But you were crouched in one position nearly the whole time...'

He drove into a small courtyard and parked the car. 'This is my place,' he said. 'I've taken a lease on a flat. It isn't very large but it's adequate for what I need at the moment. Come on up the stairs. It's on the first floor.'

His flat was one of a new development of homes that had been built about two miles from the health centre. Becky came by them on her way to work, and from what she'd heard they were up-market and sought after.

'This is the living room,' he said, opening a door and ushering her through. 'There's just the one bedroom, and a bathroom and small kitchen. It's not much, as I said, but it's enough for me. A housekeeper comes in to maintain the flats on a regular basis, and there's a caretaker who keeps an eye on security and so on. I suppose I was lucky that the lease came up just as I needed it.'

He took her hand and drew her towards a comfortable-looking settee. 'Sit down,' he said. 'I'll get something to warm you just as soon as I've lit the fire.'

He went over to the hearth, and soon there was a bright glow, orange and yellow flames flickering upwards, and heat radiated into the room. Becky took off her walking boots, flexing her toes with relief as the initial current of warmth floated towards her. Then Matthew disappeared for a moment into what must have been the bedroom and came back holding two thick sweaters. He handed one to her. 'Here, take off those damp things and put this on instead.'

She did as he suggested, pushing her arms into the soft wool and feeling the heat begin slowly to envelop her. Matthew pulled on his own sweater over his cool linen shirt, then went over to a cabinet at one side of the room.

'Brandy,' he said, handing her a glass a moment later. 'Drink it down in one go. It'll put a fire inside you.' He came and sat down beside her, swallowing his own drink and waiting until she had done the same with hers. She gave a shudder and a gasp as the liquid burned a path to her stomach. 'Good girl. That's the way,' he said, taking her empty glass from her and putting it next to his on a low table. He put his arm around her and drew her close to him, chafing her arms with his hands until she felt the blood heat within her veins and course through her body.

'That's better,' he murmured, tilting her chin so that he could look down at her face. 'There's colour in your cheeks now. I was worried; you looked so cold. Do you feel warmer now?'

'Much,' she said, conscious of his long fingers lightly pressing her jaw and feverishly aware that her soft curves were crushed against the hardness of his male body.

'I'm glad,' he said. 'I'd have hated it if anything had happened to you because of me, because I'd persuaded you into something that turned out so badly.'

'You mustn't blame yourself,' she said. 'I'm fine, really I am.' She looked up at him, feeling the golden flicker of his gaze touch her features, sliding warmly over her cheekbones, her jaw, her mouth.

She didn't know whether her lips had parted in readiness, whether she had issued a soft murmur of invitation, but she must have done, because for one fleeting, eager moment the thought crossed her mind that she would welcome the warmth of his mouth on hers, and then it was actually happening. His lips touched hers, exploring the sweet, ripe curve, tasting, sipping gently, absorbing her trembling response. His tongue flickered lightly over the fullness of her lower lip and a soft cry of need escaped her, was swallowed up in the deepening demand of his kiss.

'Ah. . . Becky,' he muttered against her throat, 'it feels so good to hold you. . .to kiss you. . .'

His breath was warm against her skin, and her toes curled as his hands stroked along the curve of her spine and meandered over the rounded line of her hip. With a muffled sigh of contentment she gave in to the sudden urge to rest her head against his chest. His arms tightened around her, and she wanted nothing more than for this moment to go on for ever, to have him hold her and to feel the slow, sweet nuzzling of his mouth against her throat.

Her arms curled about his neck, and he eased her into the soft cushions of the sofa, leaning over her, his weight shifting as he moved beside her, his lips exploring the smooth silk of her cheek, nudging aside the loose collar of her blouse beneath the deep V of the sweater. Then, as though impatient with the burden of clothes, his hand strayed beneath the wool, his palm curving over the soft mound of her breast, and suddenly she, too, ached for the touch of his hand on her bare skin.

Obligingly, he tugged the sweater from her, tossing it aside. Her breasts firmed, the nipples grazing the lace of her bra. 'You're so beautiful,' he groaned, looking down

at her, drinking in her soft curves as though he had a
raging thirst.

She moved against him, sinuously, her spine supple,
and he came down on her, easing her beneath him, sliding
his muscled length over her, so that her body blended
with the hard strength of his, and she thought she might
faint from sheer ecstasy. Her head was spinning, and a
convulsive sob hovered on her lips. Her fingers quivered
against the warm column of his throat, her head turned,
her lips tasting the clean, strong line of his jaw.

'You're trembling,' he muttered, staring down at her,
then a muffled bleeping sound came from across the
room. 'Every thought I had went out of the window as
soon as I touched you,' he muttered unevenly. He
stumbled against something on the carpet, and there was
a dull thud. She blinked, not recognising the sound at
first, then registered it as the boots she'd kicked off
earlier toppling one against the other as they met with
his feet. 'I shouldn't have started any of this. . .I should
have known better. Put your sweater back on.' He shook
his head as though to clear it.

'Why?' she said in a choked voice. 'I thought. . . Is this
because of Rachel?' She stared at him, uncomprehending.
Was he really regretting what had happened? As the hot
flood of passion began to recede a little, she cast around
for reasons why he should have had such a sudden change
of heart, but all she could think of was the expression
on his face when he had looked down at her boots on
the floor. Perhaps that was it, then—perhaps he was
thinking of the woman they belonged to. . .the woman
who had married his best friend.

His dark brows edged together. 'Rachel? She has her
own life, her own problems. I can't be there for her all
the time, even if. . .' He scowled darkly, looking about
him. 'This is here and now. What the hell is that noise?'

He moved away from her and picked something up
from the floor, stabbing at it with his finger. His jaw was

clenched, his mouth set in a hard line. The bleeping stopped suddenly, and Becky jerked in shock at the silence that fell in the room, disorientated all over again. For a while she'd been lost in another world and now reality was hitting her like a dash of cold water on her skin.

'I'm on call,' he said tersely, running a hand through his hair. 'Have been for the last half-hour. I have to answer it. I'm sorry, Becky.'

What was he apologising for? she wondered bleakly. For not wanting her enough? Or for wanting someone else more? She'd blindly given herself up to the joy of the moment, but now, facing up to what little she really knew about him, she thought it was just as well that he'd called a halt, because in days to come she could have been regretting her actions. He lived a bachelor existence, but that might not have been his choice, not if the woman he loved had married someone else, and where did that leave her?

She pulled on her sweater and ran a comb through her hair. He was jotting down details on a notepad, then he cut the call and turned back to her with a frown.

'I have to go out. Mrs Kirkwood's having breathing problems, according to the neighbour.'

'Is it bad?'

'Could be, from the sound of things. She was frail enough to begin with, and not eating didn't help. Apparently she went out in the bitter cold the other day and tried to fix a broken fence. She's an independent soul.' He sighed. 'I don't know how long I'm going to be, especially if she needs to be admitted to hospital, so I'd better drop you off at your place; it's on the way.'

'I could come with you—'

'I don't think so.' He cut her off briskly, already moving to get his medical bag, but she wasn't ready to be brushed aside so easily. She could be stubborn when

the occasion arose, and if he stayed around long enough
he'd find that out.

'You might need me, if it's a question of getting her
to hospital. She won't be happy about leaving her house.'

He grimaced, acknowledging the truth of that. 'I'll
get by.'

'I'm coming with you. We need to sort something out
if she stays determined to cope on her own once she's
recovered—the neighbour isn't always able to be there
for her, though she does her best—and maybe I can find
out if there's a relative we can call on. She talks to me.
She trusts me.'

She hoped Victoria's condition wasn't too bad and
that it wouldn't come to that, but as soon as they arrived
at the house and saw the state the old lady was in it was
clear they had no option but to arrange a hospital bed.
It was painful for her to breathe, and even though
Matthew was deft and gentle the slightest movement
caused a bout of coughing that brought up a rust-coloured
sputum.

'You're feverish too, Victoria. It's pneumonia, I'm
afraid,' Matthew said, putting away his stethoscope. 'You
need to be looked after for a while.'

'I'll arrange for someone to keep an eye on the house
for you and have it warm for when you come back,'
Becky told her, sitting by the bed and holding her hand.
'Is there anyone I can call, to come and see you while
you're in hospital—apart from your neighbour, of
course? Is there a relative at all?'

Victoria shook her head. 'Too far away,' she rasped.
'My granddaughter's the nearest, but she has her own
family to look after.'

'Do you keep in touch?'

'She writes. Comes when she can.'

There was an envelope on the bedside table, Becky
noticed. It had been opened and pushed behind the
clock. 'Is that from her? Perhaps I can get in touch.

She'll want to know what's happening, won't she?'

'Mustn't worry her. She's a sweet girl.'

'I'll just let her know where you are. Now, you just rest your head back against the pillows and I'll put a few things in an overnight bag for you.'

It was late when all the arrangements had been made and they finally stood back and saw her into the ambulance.

'I hope she'll be all right,' Becky said in a subdued voice.

'So do I.' He put an arm around her shoulders. 'Come on, I'll take you home. I've a feeling this is going to be a long night.' His mobile phone began to bleep just five minutes later.

CHAPTER SIX

THE next few days were hectic back at the centre and, disappointingly, Becky didn't see Matthew for more than a few moments at a time. He was either busy with surgery or out on call, and apart from asking her if she was fully recovered from Saturday's chill he made no mention of the time they'd spent at his flat. Perhaps he would rather push it to the back of his mind. That hurt—far more than she could ever have imagined—but life somehow went on, regardless of the way her stomach churned. She had a job to do.

She was on her way to her room when Martyn Lancaster almost collided with her. There was an air of distraction about him, not at all what she'd have expected, and she was pretty sure he hadn't been looking where he was going.

'Are you all right, Martyn? Is there something on your mind?'

'Sorry, Becky.' He gave her a rueful smile. 'I was a bit preoccupied. It's Charlotte's christening soon, and I was going over the plans for it.'

Becky's mouth curved. 'How old is she now?' she asked.

'Nine months,' Martyn answered. 'And she's beginning to take note of everything. I'm wondering if we've left this christening a bit too late, to be honest, but we thought December would suit most people. . .just before Christmas and all the family would be able to come. We thought perhaps she'd be old enough not to be crying all the while. We're planning on having a christening party back at the house in a couple of weeks. Will you be able to come, do you think?'

120

'I'd love to,' Becky told him with a smile. 'How is Daniel getting on with her these days?'

'You might well ask,' Martyn laughed. 'He thinks his sister's OK as sisters go, I suppose, but he's started school now, and I think he's cottoned onto the idea that his mum's at home with the baby most of the time. He's not too sure he's happy about that.'

'I expect Sarah makes a big fuss of him, though, to make up for it,' Becky murmured, and Martyn grinned.

'She does. He'll be all right; we'll see to that. Must rush.' He strode cheerfully on down the corridor and Becky made her way to her own room.

Blood tests were first on the agenda today and already the waiting room was beginning to fill up. She called the first patient and worked her way smoothly through her list.

She recognised Alan Cole from the diabetes clinic. He was a youngish man in his late twenties and he hadn't been at all happy with the diagnosis, she remembered, nor with the advice that Matthew had given him—that he should try to lose a little weight.

'How are you, Mr Cole?' She glanced at his notes. 'Dr Kingston wants you to have a blood test so that we can see how things are going with the blood sugar.'

'That's what he said.' Alan shrugged. 'What with diets and blood tests, if it's not one thing it's another, and on top of that I need to go to the optician now.'

Becky glanced at him as she dealt with his form. 'Are you having trouble with your eyes?'

'Well, these glasses don't seem to be any good any more. I only had them a year ago, and I shouldn't need a new pair yet, but I can't cope with them as they are.'

'What seems to be the problem?'

He made an irritable gesture with his hands. 'Everything keeps blurring, and I can't focus properly with these. It's a damn nuisance. I shall have to get them changed, but I've got better things to do with my time than keep shifting about from one appointment to another.'

Becky studied him thoughtfully. 'Perhaps you ought to wait for a while until we have your diabetes stabilised.'

The man frowned. 'What's that got to do with it?' he muttered impatiently.

'Well, the fluctuations that you are having with your blood-sugar levels can cause problems with your eyes. You might find it best to wait until we have things under control and until you've been stabilised for at least a month, before you go after new glasses.'

'I can't see what my blood has to do with my having glasses.'

'It sounds odd, doesn't it?' Becky answered him. 'But if you get a new pair of glasses now you might find that they're no good after a month or so. It could turn out to be quite costly for you.'

'I still don't see why I can't get my eyes seen to. I can't work properly if my sight's giving me trouble, and the optician should know his job well enough to be able to sort me out.'

'Perhaps it would be a good idea for you to see Dr Kingston again and talk to him about the problem. He can advise you.' Becky finished taking the blood sample and pressed a cotton-wool ball to his arm. 'All done,' she said, putting the sample bottles to one side. Inspecting the site, she threw the cotton-wool ball into the bin and Alan Cole began to pull down his sleeve. He shrugged into his jacket, frowning.

'Well, I hope there aren't going to be too many more of those,' he said, on his way out.

If Matthew had been in surgery, she would have gone along to talk to him now, but he was out on call, and so she watched Alan Cole walk away without saying any more. She'd let Matthew know about the situation, though. He might be able to get through to him where she had failed.

Alan Cole had been her last patient for blood tests that morning and she took advantage of the lull to go off and leave a note on Matthew's desk. He'd be coming into the surgery around six this evening, but she'd be on her way home by then.

It felt odd, somehow, walking into his empty room. She'd have liked to have been able to stay and talk to him, just for a moment, and she hadn't been prepared for this aching void that opened up like a chasm inside her. Yet it had been happening more and more just lately. When he wasn't around, she found she missed him terribly; she'd started to listen for the sound of his voice, to watch for the merest hint of a smile.

'Fool,' she told herself. 'You're asking for trouble. . . falling for a man who doesn't even begin to feel the same way about you.'

She sighed. The way she was headed, she could finish up being badly hurt. That possibility had never occurred to her before. In all the time she'd known Drew, she had never once felt like this. The thought washed over her in a guilty tide. Drew must be back by now, and she ought to ring him, but she'd been putting it off, because it was going to be hard to say what she had to say. There was no future for them.

Ever since she had known Matthew, her life had been turned upside down, her emotions swinging from one extreme to the other, but there was going to be no happy ending for her there either.

Matthew had kissed her, and there was no doubting that he wanted her, but what did that mean? Absolutely nothing. They'd been thrown together through their work, and he'd behaved like any other red-blooded male might, given the opportunity. Only, he had seemed to draw back from her, and she was in a state of complete confusion.

There were too many reasons why their relationship wouldn't work. There was Sophie, for a start. He knew that she had ties that were binding, ties that any man might find restrictive. And then—the thought came like a blow—he had loved Rachel. Had he ever recovered from that? He had loved and lost, and anyone else might fade in comparison. Yet he had turned to her. Why? What did he want from her? An affair, no strings?

She damped down another heavy sigh. It had been a mistake to get involved, to let herself get tangled in such an emotional web. All she could do now was immerse herself in work, and try to push away these unwelcome thoughts.

She went home later that day in an oddly subdued mood. Sophie would be staying late at school, taking part in preparations for the Christmas production, and the silence that met her in the house made her feel unusually restless.

Glancing around the living room, she came to a decision. Work was what she needed, something to take her mind off things, and she'd been putting off the last of the decorating for long enough. She had the paper and the paste, and what better time was there to get on with it?

She changed quickly into snug-fitting jeans and an old shirt that had seen better days, then she went downstairs and mixed the paste. A couple of days ago, in a burst of energy, she'd stripped the walls of paper, but with one thing and another she hadn't had time to finish the job. It was well overdue.

The room was a straightforward enough one to tackle and after an hour or so she stood back for a moment to survey her handiwork. She hadn't made bad progress, all things considered. Then the doorbell rang, shattering the quiet, and she glanced at her watch. It was too soon for Sophie and, anyway, she had a key. Who else could it be? Wiping her hands on a cloth, she went to open the door.

Matthew stood there, dressed in casual clothes rather than one of the suits he wore for work. Well-cut trousers moulded his long legs and she could see that he was wearing a sweater beneath his jacket.

'Matthew,' she said, 'I wasn't expecting—' She broke off. She had been thinking about him all day and now to have him turn up on the doorstep, looking fiendishly attractive, made her throat close and her mouth go dry. She slid the chain back and held the door open. 'Come in.'

'Thanks. Am I interrupting anything?' he asked, his glance skimming over her. 'Your meal, perhaps?'

Becky shook her head, leading him through the living room towards the kitchen. 'I haven't eaten yet, apart from a quick snack. I was in the middle of decorating, to be honest. Sophie isn't due home yet. . .she's painting scenery for the school play. . .and I thought I'd take advantage of the time and get on with something. That's why I look such a mess.'

Self-consciously, she ran her hands down her jeans. Her hair must be wild and there were probably smudges of paste on her face. Why did he have to see her like this, why couldn't she have been dressed up, fresh from the shower? It wasn't fair—the one time he'd come visiting and she had to look a total wreck.

His glance roamed over her, taking in the soft swell of her breasts beneath the cotton shirt, and the curve of her hips where the denim clung faithfully.

'You could never look a mess if you tried. You look absolutely gorgeous, if the truth be known—apart from this tiny smudge of paste. . .' A smile tugged at his mouth, his fingers coming up to trail lightly over her cheek, leaving her flushed and breathless.

'I've been up to my eyes in wallpaper and paste,' she said huskily. 'I'm probably covered in the stuff.'

He grinned wryly and removed a thin strip of paper from her shirt, before looking around at her efforts. 'When we first met, you said decorating wasn't your strong point, but from the looks of things you seem to be getting on well enough with this.'

'I helped my father a few times, so I know roughly what to do. This is the first time I've tackled it on my own, though. I was just about to take a break. Can I get you something to drink? Tea, coffee, or something stronger?'

'A coffee would go down well, thanks.'

They walked into the kitchen, where Becky switched on the coffee pot. 'Have you just come from the surgery? I know you had a late list.'

'I had a batch of well-person checks to fit in,' he told her. 'They couldn't be done in normal surgery hours. That's how this entire week seems to have gone, with emergencies and things having to be fitted in alongside the usual run of events. I feel as though I haven't had a moment to breathe since the weekend.'

He paused, leaning against one of the kitchen units. 'Actually, I stopped by to thank you for leaving the note about Alan Cole. He seems to be having problems adjusting to being diagnosed diabetic, and I think maybe we should have him in at the next clinic rather than wait until he's due to come in. I've organised an appointment for him. He hadn't mentioned the problem with his eyes but he probably didn't see the connection until you pointed it out.'

'I don't think he sees the connection even now,' Becky said with a faint grin. 'I don't think he was ready to take my word for it, but an explanation coming from you will probably make all the difference.'

'We'll see, anyway. The other reason I stopped by is to tell you about a half-day lecture session on diabetes that's coming up soon at the Royal. Professor Hammond will be the main speaker and I thought you might like to go along with me. We'd have to clear it with Martyn, of course, but I can't see any problem there.'

So he hadn't stopped by simply to see her. A small wave of disappointment washed over her, but she said simply, 'Sounds fine by me. I'm glad of the chance to keep up to date.' She handed him a coffee. 'Talking of the Royal, I haven't had a chance to ask you, but have you heard anything about how Madge is? She took a nasty fall and she was pretty shocked.'

'They operated, as we'd expected. The bone had to be pinned, and there was several hours' delay before a theatre was free, which is never a good thing. The sooner hip fractures are dealt with the better, but at least she's comfortable now. She's had trouble with her hip before, but she's a stubborn woman and the more people tell her to take things easier, the more determined she is to keep active. I think she'll be all right, given time, though she'll need a fair amount of physiotherapy. I went to see her at lunchtime today, as a matter of fact, and she seemed cheerful enough. She was chafing at the bit because she's stuck in hospital.'

'I can imagine. She seemed such a lively person when I met her, and I'm sure she won't like being restricted. It was thoughtful of you to go and visit her.'

'I checked on Victoria Kirkwood while I was there. She's doing OK, and they're probably going to let her come home again soon. Apparently you managed to sorted out something with the granddaughter so that she'll be looked after?'

'Yes, I managed to get in touch and explain the problem. She was happy to help out.' It gave her a warm feeling inside, to know that Matthew had followed through, but that was one of the things she liked about him—that he cared about people, they weren't just patients to him, and he made time for them. In the short time he'd been at the centre, he'd made a lot of friends. 'Your patients will miss you when you go,' she said. *She* would miss him, but she wasn't going to dwell on that.

He glanced at her, a dark brow lifting. 'What brought that on?'

'You did,' she murmured, 'just by being you.'

'I'm flattered, I think. . .but they'll take to my replacement just as well, I imagine.'

'You wouldn't think of staying on?' She'd said it before she'd had time to think, but he was already shaking his head.

'Martyn suggested it a while ago, but I've already signed the agreement with the new practice. It would be too costly to back down—and besides, the facilities there are second to none.'

She hadn't really expected anything else. He swallowed the last of his coffee and pushed his cup to one side, glancing through the open door to the living room. 'This isn't getting your decorating done, is it? You've only a couple of walls still to do in there. Do you want a hand to finish it?'

'You're offering?' Her brows lifted.

'Why not? Between the two of us we should soon see it off.'

She grinned. 'I never turn down an offer of help,' she told him. 'I hope you meant it.'

'Of course I meant it.' He smiled at her and her heart gave a funny little leap in her chest, banging against her ribcage. 'Shall we get on with this paper-hanging, then?' he suggested.

Becky eyed his clothes with a slight grimace. 'You're not exactly dressed for it,' she said. 'Perhaps it isn't such a good idea after all.'

'Let me worry about that.' He was already taking off his jacket and placing it over the back of the chair. Then he peeled off his sweater and she watched the rippling interplay of muscle and bone and was swamped by a compelling urge to run her hands over him. It was such a strong instinct that she blushed and went hot all over and had to turn away and make a pretence of clearing away the cups.

Thankfully he didn't seem to notice her distraction, and he walked through to the living room and cast an

eye over the paste table and the rolls of paper. 'Do you
want to cut and paste?' he asked. 'And I'll do the hanging. I can, perhaps, reach better than you.'

It seemed a practical idea. She'd struggled, balancing
precariously on the rickety stepladder, but he made it
seem like an effortless task. He was sure-footed, physi-
cally in peak form, and he seemed to have a never ending
supply of energy. They worked as a team, efficiently,
smoothly, as though they did this sort of thing every day,
and in less than a couple of hours she was handing him
the last sheet and he was sliding it into place, brushing
it lightly, with practised ease. She stood back and
watched him make the finishing touches.

'That's it, then,' he said, a cheerful grin pulling at his
mouth. 'We made short work of that, didn't we? Perhaps
we should go into business together.' He surveyed their
handiwork from the stepladder, then turned back towards
her, leaning slightly forwards, his arms supported along
the top bar of the ladder.

She smiled up at him. 'I'd have been working on that
all night if it hadn't been for you.'

'You would,' he said, and there was a devilish twist
to his mouth. 'I think I ought to claim my reward,
don't you?'

'Reward?' she echoed, and her heart began to thump
in response to the gleaming promise she read in his eyes.
Slowly, he came down from the ladder and stood in
front of her, reaching out and drawing her ever closer
towards him.

'Can you blame me?' he queried softly. 'When you
look at me like that, with those beautiful wide blue eyes,
it takes all I've got to keep from touching you. . .and
then I wonder why I'm even struggling with myself,
when it seems to me that you have such a kissable
mouth. . .'

And the next moment she was in his arms and he had
claimed her mouth with his own, igniting a fire in her

that threatened to burn out of control. His hand rested
on the curve of her hip, then slid upward to cup her
breast, his thumb gliding over the soft mound, a groan
breaking in his throat as the nipple surged and hardened
beneath his fingers.

'I want you,' he muttered thickly. 'You've no idea
just how much. . .'

She trembled, her whole body quivering with need and
longing, an ache of desire growing in her, but just as her
hands trailed upwards to explore the muscled strength of
his arms he drew back a little, holding her still. She
didn't understand what was happening, why his mood
had changed, but he was frowning now, his face serious,
his mouth firm and straight.

'Matthew—'

'I thought I heard a door,' he said flatly. 'Are you
expecting Sophie back yet?'

She sucked in a breath. 'I'd forgotten. . .' How could
she have been so blinded to everything? Footsteps
sounded in the hall, and Matthew grimaced, straightening
and pushing her away from him. Becky felt her heart
sink as his expression cooled, and then Sophie came into
the room, stopping to toss her bag down onto a chair,
staring from one to the other.

'I thought someone must be here,' she said. 'I saw the
car outside.' She was guarded in the way she spoke, and
in the way she looked at Matthew. 'I didn't mean
to interrupt anything. Don't mind me; I'll go up to
my room.'

She turned to go back out again and Becky said
quickly, 'You don't have to do that.' Sophie was sensitive
to the fact that she was intruding on something, but
whether she was aware of exactly what she'd interrupted
was another matter. 'You don't have to shut yourself
away,' Becky added.

She was conscious of Matthew's taut figure by her
side and she wondered what he felt at being interrupted.

This was Sophie's home, though, as much as it was her own, and she didn't want her driven away, whatever the reason.

'Perhaps I should go,' he said, and she knew an aching sense of despair. She'd been through this before, with Drew, but there was no easy answer to the situation, was there? Those few close moments were lost now, and weren't likely to be recaptured.

'Because of me?' Sophie guessed. 'There's no need.'

'How are you coping these days?' Matthew said, glancing at her. 'Are you keeping up with the injections and so on?'

Sophie shrugged. 'I don't really have much choice, do I?'

'Not if you want to keep out of hospital.' His grin was rueful. 'Do you belong to any kind of diabetic group?'

Sophie shook her head. 'Becky suggested it, but none of my friends are diabetics and I didn't see the point.'

'You might find you'd make more friends,' Matthew suggested calmly. 'It isn't just a question of craft fairs and the like, to raise money; there are discos as well from time to time. I've a lot to do with the local group, so I could let you know when they come up, if you like.'

'I could always give it a try, I suppose,' Sophie said, in an offhanded fashion, 'provided I had nothing else to do.' She wasn't giving anything away, still keeping herself locked inside her prickly defences, and Becky felt like shaking her, because this wasn't the real Sophie, and she wondered whether the sweet girl she really was would ever surface again.

'I'm going to get supper ready,' she murmured, then turned to Matthew and asked, 'Will you eat with us?'

He shook his head. 'I don't want to put you to any trouble,' he said.

'It's no trouble and it's the least I can do after you stayed and helped me. One less TV dinner? Provided, of course, that my cooking doesn't put you off.' She grinned at him mischievously and he sent her a rueful smile.

'That wasn't fair. OK, you win.'

Sophie hovered by the door and glanced around. 'You've finished it,' she said. 'Wow.'

'Not on my own. What do you think of it?'

'It looks good,' Sophie admitted. She turned to go out of the room. 'I'll be down in a while. I want to change out of these things and I must have a shower; I think I've got paint streaked in my hair.'

Left alone once more with Matthew, Becky was conscious of the odd little silence that fell between them. 'I should go and see to the meal,' she said. 'We'll eat in the kitchen; I hope you don't mind.' She headed in that direction and left him to put his sweater back on and follow her there.

'Why should I mind? It suits me fine. It's cosy in here, you've made it very homely.' He watched as she moved a bowl of chrysanthemums from the table.

'They're from the garden,' she told him. 'There's a small greenhouse, but I haven't had much time yet to get it organised.'

'That's what I miss, having just a flat,' he said. 'All I have are a few indoor plants that people have given to me, but it's convenient where I am at the moment. Once I'm settled at the new practice I'll take time to look around for a property that's more suitable.' His words struck a chill round her heart. For just a while, she'd managed to forget that he would be leaving. She turned away to open the fridge door, biting down on her lip.

He watched her as she moved about the kitchen making preparations for the meal. 'Is there anything I can do to help?'

She glanced towards the wine rack. 'You could open a bottle of wine if you like,' she said, putting on a bright tone. 'I think we deserve a glass of plonk, don't you, after all our hard work? There should be a corkscrew in one of the drawers.'

Matthew viewed the honeyed chicken she had prepared, now under the grill, and selected a bottle. 'You're a very efficient person, aren't you, Becky?' he murmured with a faint smile, watching her deftly tossing a salad. 'Nothing ever seems to flummox you. You just move smoothly through life, dealing with everything that comes your way. You must be a very strong minded person.'

'Strong. . .me? I hadn't thought about it,' she said, laying out cutlery on the table.

'I think you are,' he said. 'You've been through a lot, but you wouldn't know it, looking at you. Everything about you is neatly contained, absorbed, organised. I've never met anyone quite like you.'

He was looking at her curiously, taking in the slight flush of her cheeks, the sudden confused softening of her mouth, and she stopped what she was doing for a moment, returning his gaze.

'I'm not sure what brought this on,' she said wryly, but he was still looking at her mouth and she had the strong feeling that he was thinking back to those moments in the living room, when he had kissed her.

He put down the bottle of wine and came around the table towards her. 'It felt so good,' he said huskily, 'having you in my arms. I'd quite like to repeat the exercise some time.'

He was very close to her now and she felt a heady throb of excitement race through her bloodstream, sending a ripple of heat over her skin. He wasn't touching her, but her body tingled in delicious anticipation, until Sophie walked into the room and the moment was shattered. Matthew drew away from her and sent a flickering glance towards her sister.

Sophie's grey eyes were cool, her thoughts shuttered behind a blank expression.

Becky drew in a steadying breath. 'Supper's ready.'

'I could take mine up to my room,' Sophie said. 'I've some homework to do.'

Becky shook her head, pushing away the tempting thought of what it might be like to have more time alone with Matthew. 'I don't think it's a good idea for you to keep shutting yourself away up there. I want you to eat with us and I'm sure your homework can wait until another night. You've spent hours helping out at school, as it is.'

She was aware of Matthew's narrow glance skimming over her as she spoke, and she felt the tension rise within her. Sophie shrugged and took her place at the table. 'Leave her to get on with it,' Drew would have said. 'That's what teenagers do.' Was that what Matthew was thinking now? But it didn't feel right to her, and even though Matthew probably shared Drew's sentiments this was something she didn't want to compromise on. She had to follow her own instincts, and instinct told her that Sophie needed the security of being included.

She set the meal out on the table and Matthew poured wine before going to take his place. She couldn't be sure what he was thinking but when he turned to Sophie he spoke in an even tone, his features composed.

'Becky tells me you've been painting scenery,' he said. 'How does that work—do you do your own piece or do you just fill in someone else's design?'

'We just have to block in areas of colour,' Sophie told him. 'Some of the teachers drew the backcloth, and our bit was quite simple really.'

'From what I've seen of your work,' Matthew said, 'you could probably have drawn some of the backcloth yourself. You're really very talented. Are you going to make a career of art? With the right qualification, you could go far.'

Sophie brushed off the compliment. 'That would take several years, though.'

'Does that matter?'

'I think it does. I'm not sure I want to wait that long to gain my independence. I'd like to get a flat of my own, or share with a friend.'

'That sounds like a reasonable ambition to me.'

Becky shot him a taut glance. 'Don't encourage her.'

'Why not? Most people want to be independent some time.'

'She's too young.'

'I'm not that young,' Sophie intervened. 'I could do it in a few weeks, after my birthday. It only needs Becky's consent, but she won't give it. I don't see why. I have money of my own, in trust, and all she has to do is sign a form and agree to let me have some of it.'

She was turning to Matthew for support, and Becky cut in firmly, 'Why do you think I've spent so much time trying to make this place into a home? It was for you, a fresh start, but you've hardly given it a chance.'

'I didn't ask you to. All I'm asking is that you give me the chance to take charge of my own life.'

'Let's not get into a discussion of that right now, Sophie,' Becky said. 'This isn't the time or place.'

Matthew shot her a cool glance, and she registered it with angry resentment. She wasn't going to be undermined in this. He might disagree with the stand she was taking, but she would be the one who was left to pick up the pieces when Sophie made a mess of her life.

Sophie's mouth set in a tight line. It was an awkward meal after that, not at all what Becky would have planned, and as soon as they'd finished coffee Sophie took herself stiffly off to her room. Matthew watched her go.

'You think I'm wrong, don't you?' Becky said, her tone curt.

'I was under the impression you weren't interested in my opinion,' he returned crisply. 'You've decided what's right for her, and you don't intend to argue about it.'

'It's difficult enough for me to keep her on the straight

and narrow, without having other people encourage her in her wild ideas.'

'You're so sure that's what I would have done? Don't you think you should have given me credit for having some tact and diplomacy?'

'I thought—'

'You assumed I was going to agree with everything she said,' he cut in. 'You were so sure that I would say the wrong thing.'

'I can't afford to take the chance. She's young and vulnerable, and I have to deal with her, day in and day out. I'm responsible for her, not just for the next month or so but until she's of age, and probably beyond. Didn't you think of that? In a few weeks' time you won't even be around.'

His mouth tightened. 'I hadn't forgotten.' He stood up. 'The meal was delicious, thank you, but I should be making tracks now. I've some patients' notes I want to go through before tomorrow morning.'

She knew he liked to spend time acquainting himself with patients' records. It was one of the things she respected about him, the way he took time to delve into things more deeply so that he wouldn't miss anything, but this time she suspected it was just an excuse. Everything had gone wrong. She'd antagonised him, and now he was cold, almost like a stranger towards her.

She saw him to the door but he made no attempt to kiss her again and walked briskly away to his car. She watched him go before turning back into the hall, fighting down a feeling of desolation that threatened to overwhelm her.

CHAPTER SEVEN

SHE didn't see much of Matthew in the next few days, and her emotions swung through the disturbing extremes of wanting to keep a safe distance between them and needing to be with him.

December had brought with it cold winds and bright mornings, when a white layer of frost covered everything. She walked to work one morning, banging her hands together to keep the circulation going, her breath freezing on the air.

She arrived at the centre at the same time as Matthew, and he held open the main door for her, waiting while she stamped her feet briskly on the mat.

'Not the best day for walking to work,' he said. 'What's happened to your car?'

'It hasn't been running too well,' she told him. 'I thought I'd have it checked over before winter sets in properly. It always gets sluggish with the cold weather.' She studied him keenly, searching his features for just a glimpse of the old warmth. Had it only been a few days since he'd kissed her and told her how much he wanted her? She'd missed the gentle, caring man he'd been more than she cared to admit. Try as she might to stand alone and fill her life with other things, just lately he always seemed to be uppermost in her thoughts.

Now, as they walked through to Reception, she said, 'I looked for you the last two afternoons. . .there were some papers you needed to deal with, and some notes. I'm afraid your tray seems to be filling up rapidly.'

'I'll look at them as soon as I get the chance,' he said. 'I've had to go over to my new practice on a couple of occasions this week. There are things I need to organise there and I've had to attend one or two meetings to make sure everything's set up all right for when I start.'

'I expect you're wishing you could get on with it, aren't you?' she commented, keeping her tone carefully matter of fact. Somehow she had to shore up her defences. With every day that passed, he was distancing himself from her.

'In a way. As the new year comes closer I'm beginning to feel more and more impatient.'

'That's understandable. You said the facilities were second to none,' she murmured.

He nodded. 'A new wing's been added where we'll be able to hold antenatal clinics and deal especially with diabetic patients who need extra care during pregnancy. Since that's my speciality it's bound to appeal. There's room for visiting consultants too.' He was checking his list of appointments as they spoke but now he glanced at her and asked coolly, 'How's Sophie these days? She looked well enough the other day. Is she adjusting any better now?'

'I think so,' Becky answered him. 'I think the whole episode of going into hospital frightened her a little, though she hasn't talked about it much. I think Rebeccah scolded her a bit and told her what a silly girl she'd been, but it's a job getting her to talk about anything seriously for long.'

'A typical teenager,' he remarked, reaching for a file and scanning the documents.

'I suppose so.' She hoped that was all it was, but Sophie hadn't been quite her usual self for some time now, and it was worrying not knowing exactly what was the root cause. Until she knew that, she couldn't begin to deal with the problem properly, and Sophie wasn't providing any clues.

She glanced at her own appointments book as Martyn Lancaster came into the office. He was carrying a file and as he looked across at Matthew he took out one of the papers and handed it to him.

'We've received confirmation on that course you were asking about,' he said. 'I managed to book a place for Becky too. I agree with you—it would be a good idea if you could both go along. I've made all the arrangements for people to fill in for you tomorrow afternoon, so there's no problem there.' He gave Becky a sheet with details of the lecture topics, and she studied it for a while, until she became conscious that the waiting room was filling up rapidly and there was work to be done.

The morning progressed smoothly, but she didn't see Matthew again until after lunch, when she was scheduled to assist him in the diabetes clinic. His mood was brittle, and her hopes of spending a few moments chatting with him before they set to work rapidly faded as he reached for the afternoon's post and skimmed quickly through it.

His cool detachment hurt, but she determined not to let it bother her as she ushered in their first patient. The woman was obviously troubled, biting her lip as Matthew greeted her and then went back to his study of the report from the eye clinic.

'How are you, Joan?' Becky asked. 'It's a month since we saw you last, isn't it, but you've been to the hospital in between times?'

Joan nodded. 'I don't understand what's happening,' she said, dropping her voice in an urgent undertone. 'This business with my eyes—it's very worrying.'

'I'm sure Dr Kingston will explain things to you,' Becky said soothingly, 'but at least your diabetes is under control now, which means that any problems should be limited.'

Matthew looked up from the paper he was studying. 'Unfortunately these things happen sometimes. If there are too many fluctuations in blood-sugar control and if they last over a period of time, then the blood vessels at the back of the eye can be affected. In your case it looks as though we can treat this, but it will mean going into hospital to have the condition corrected, using a laser. It's a treatment that can be very effective.'

While Becky dealt with the forms that had to be filled in, Matthew carefully answered Mrs Barstow's questions, and after a few minutes more she left the room looking a deal happier than she had when she'd come in.

Their next patient wasn't quite so easy to deal with. Edna Carlisle's feet were giving cause for concern, with calluses and cracked skin giving her a lot of discomfort.

'Sometimes there are patches that go numb,' she told Matthew. 'I told the doctor at the hospital about it but he kept mumbling on about my giving up smoking. What's that got to do with my feet?'

Matthew grimaced. 'It does seem an odd thing to say, doesn't it? But he was right, I'm afraid. The problem with smoking is that it can lead to narrowing of the arteries in later life and then you can end up with circulatory problems. In your case you're already having trouble with your feet. We can help a little with that by referring you to a chiropodist but what you need to do is to cut out the cigarettes and try to make sure that you wear comfortable shoes. Not ones that are going to pinch you or cause you any more problems than you already have.'

'I think we could try and fit you in with the chiropodist this afternoon,' Becky told her when Matthew had finished his examination. 'I'll take you over to her room now if you like, and explain the situation. We're very lucky in having chiropody on the premises.'

When she came back a few moments later, Matthew was glancing through the next patient's notes on the computer screen.

'We wouldn't have half these problems,' he said, 'if patients would only do the sensible thing right from the beginning.'

'A lot of people abuse their health,' she agreed, 'or take unnecessary risks, and all the talking in the world doesn't seem to make a deal of difference. Which reminds me, I meant to ask about your friend Madge. How is she? Is she out of hospital yet? I heard there were complications—an ulcer that was resisting treatment.'

'I think it's responding now. When I saw her at lunch-time she told me they might be sending her home any day. Her physiotherapy's going well enough, though she keeps on complaining because she isn't fully active yet, but that's typical of Madge.'

'You've visited several times, haven't you? Her husband popped into the surgery earlier this week and told me that you'd been in to see her again.'

'I was at the hospital anyway.'

'Oh?' She glanced at him questioningly, and he paused, turning away from the screen.

'Steve, Rachel's husband, was admitted for chemo-therapy last week, and I went to see him.' He grimaced. 'He has Hodgkin's disease.'

'Oh, no. . .I'm so sorry. . .I didn't know.' Becky was completely taken aback by the news, and mortified that she'd gone stumbling in without thinking. Matthew looked so weary and fed up that she wanted to reach out to him, to put her arms around him. She'd nursed patients with malignancy of the lymphatic tissues, and she knew how devastating the diagnosis could be, the effect it had on the men and their families and friends as long as the uncertainty of the outcome existed.

'Why should you know? I didn't tell anyone, and Rachel hasn't said a lot because she doesn't want the children upset. She just needs me to be there to help her through it.'

'It must be hard for her—for you too. I can understand how you must be feeling.'

'You can't.' His sharp tone made her flinch. 'How can you begin to imagine how I feel? He's been my friend for as long as I can remember. We did everything together before. . .'

'Before you knew Rachel? I heard you were thinking of marrying her at one time.'

'Who told you that?' He seemed angry, his eyes darkening, a muscle jerking spasmodically in his jaw.

'I'm sorry, I didn't mean—'

'It was someone from the club, I suppose. They had no right. It was private. It had nothing to do with anyone. Haven't they anything better to do than spread gossip?' His teeth clenched and she stared at him, shocked by his vehemence. It had happened so long ago, yet it still had the power to disturb him.

'No one meant any harm by it,' she said quietly.

'They never do.' He was silent for a moment, abstracted, then he straightened and went back to studying the notes. 'Perhaps we ought to have the next patient in,' he said briskly. 'We've a long list this afternoon.'

She clamped her mouth shut. She had to accept his dismissal of the subject, even though it hurt to see his pain. How could she do otherwise? It was no wonder that he had seemed preoccupied, when he had so much to cause him concern, and it was selfish of her to hope she might feature even in a small part of his life. And he was right, of course—there wasn't time to talk, not when they had patients waiting.

She worked efficiently for the rest of the afternoon and she didn't make the mistake again of mixing business with anything else. Her manner was nothing if not professional.

'Who have we next?' he asked.

'Alex Bailey, fourteen years old.' She handed him a thin folder of documents and went to show the boy and his mother in.

'You seem to be getting along just fine, young man,' Matthew told him. 'The test results are all excellent, so you must be doing the right thing. How are you finding the injections?'

Alex shrugged. 'OK, I suppose, but I'm a bit sore on my thigh.'

'Yes, I noticed that,' Matthew said. 'Do you always inject in the same place?'

The boy nodded.

'Perhaps you could vary the sites a bit,' Matthew said. 'Try your tummy, perhaps. Or, if you don't mind asking your mother to help out occasionally, you could try the upper arm—I know it might be difficult for you to inject yourself there. But there are other parts that can be injected as well, you know. . . If you use the same place over and over again, then eventually the skin will thicken, as you've discovered. Otherwise, you're doing very well. I'm very pleased with you.'

'I had a picture of what bits to inject, but I lost it,' Alex said, looking sheepish, 'so I carried on doing them in the same place. I know I should have taken better care of the information pack, but it sort of got scattered about.'

'It's no problem,' Becky told him. 'I can always get you another one. I've a drawer full of spare packs and leaflets in the filing cabinet over there. Any time you feel you want me to explain things again or go over something you've forgotten, just ask. You're doing so well, we want you to keep up the good work.'

The boy's mother smiled. 'He's been much better these last few months, and he's been able to join in with games and everything at school without any difficulty. I'm really proud of him.'

'So you should be,' Matthew told her.

Mother and son left the room after a few more minutes, and Becky started to tidy up, moving jerkily about the room, conscious of being alone with Matthew at last, but uneasy about the void that had grown between them. She didn't know how to bridge it, how to get back to the warm relationship they'd had before.

'Are there any more waiting to be seen?' he asked.

'They were the last,' she said shortly.

'That didn't take as long as I thought it would.' He
pushed back his chair and went over to the window, and
she looked at him, watching him stretch his arms as
though easing the tension in his limbs.

She averted her gaze. She finished tidying her cupboards and would have gone from the room, only
Matthew stopped her at the door.

'I didn't mean to be brusque earlier,' he said. 'It was
boorish of me, because none of this is your fault. It's
just that I need to concentrate on what I'm doing when
I'm with the patients, and there's been such a lot to
distract me lately.'

'I can imagine.' Her tone was curt. The woman he
loved was upset because of her husband and she had
turned immediately to him. Jealousy seared her to the
core, leaving her full of guilt.

'Can you?' he murmured. 'Look, I'm sorry if I
snapped. I know you deserve better than that.' He smiled
briefly—a weary kind of smile that made her heart go
out to him—and when his glance moved over her in an
unspoken question she went to him, letting him draw her
into his arms. Maybe it was just comfort he wanted at
that moment, another warm, human presence, but that
didn't matter. Somehow, in these last few weeks, she
had learned what love was all about, and she knew that
if he was to ask her she would always be here for him.

His hands circled her waist, pulling her close. 'You're
such a restful person, Becky,' he said. 'You should have
so much more from life. . .'

She placed a finger on his mouth, cutting off the words,
and he brushed his lips along its length, bending his head
towards her so that his cheek lightly grazed her own.
Her palms slid down, smoothing over his shoulders, and
she wished his jacket wasn't in the way, so that she could
feel the warmth of him as well as the strength of muscle
and bone.

'I have all I need,' she murmured softly. 'At least, for

the moment.' And he kissed her then, tenderly, the very gentleness of that caress making her heart swell with longing, so that when he finally released her she stared up at him, bemused, her lips tingling as though he'd touched them with fire.

Then, in the next moment, the door was pushed open and a small boy walked into the room. Her scattered wits reassembled, and she studied the grubby little urchin, who surveyed her with equal interest. He looked about five years old and had bright fair hair, and right now his hands were smudged with grime and his grey trousers were torn at the knee.

'Who is this?' she asked, pretending not to recognise Dr Lancaster's little boy. 'Who is it under all that grubbiness? It can't be Daniel, can it?'

Daniel grinned at her. 'Of course it's me,' he said matter-of-factly. 'Who else would it be?' His glance went from Becky to Matthew. 'Were you two kissing?' he asked.

Becky choked and Matthew hid a grin, hurrying to the rescue, thumping her on the back. 'Whatever gave you that idea?'

Daniel's shoulders lifted in a careless gesture. 'Just wondered,' he said. 'I fell over and hurt my knee. Mummy said to come and find you.'

'Isn't your mummy with you?' Becky asked, but just then Sarah Lancaster popped her head round the door.

'There he is. I have to have eyes in the back of my head to keep up with this one. He fell over on the way back from school,' she explained. 'Would you mind having a look at him for me? Only, I need to take Charlotte over to the health visitor before she finishes for the day. I want a quick word with her. Would you mind? He knows about the sweet jar, by the way, so I've promised him you'll let him choose one when he's been cleaned up.'

'Of course. Leave him with us,' Becky reassured her.

'Thanks. You're a life-saver.'

Sarah disappeared again and Becky turned back to Daniel. 'Right, young man,' she said, 'sit on the chair while I find the cotton wool.'

Matthew handed her a kidney bowl and as her glance met his she saw the faint rueful twist to his mouth. Carefully she rolled back Daniel's trouser leg and surveyed the damage.

'There's a lot of grit in there,' she told him. 'I'll wash it ever so carefully. All right?' Daniel nodded soberly. 'You're being a very brave boy,' she said, and he nodded again.

'It doesn't hurt nearly as much as when I banged my head at school. I cried when I did that, but I was only little then,' he added hurriedly.

Becky cleaned him up and put a small dressing on the wound. 'Mummy can take that off when you get home,' she told him when she'd finished and he was inspecting the contents of the sweet jar. 'We'd better go and see if we can find her.'

They went along to the health visitor's room, and when they'd deposited Daniel back with his mother Becky walked with Matthew towards the main door.

'I'll give you a lift home,' he said.

He was quiet after that, his thoughts turned inward, and she hesitated a second or two before venturing softly, 'Did you have any plans for this evening? I could make dinner for us, if you like.'

He shook his head. 'I don't think so,' he said flatly. 'Anyway, I wouldn't be much company for you today.'

'You don't need to be anything other than yourself,' she murmured, but from the rigid set of his features she knew he wasn't going to be persuaded to change his mind.

They reached his car, and he let her into the passenger side, saying, 'I'll be busy this evening. There are things I need to get on with.'

She tried not to flinch at the blunt rejection, but she felt the sting of tears behind her eyelids all the same. Was it really any more than she had expected? That earlier closeness seemed to have vanished, and perhaps she'd been foolish to look for anything more.

'As you please,' she murmured as he set the car in motion. 'It was just a thought.'

He touched her arm gently. 'Don't be offended, Becky, I didn't mean to hurt you. I'll see you tomorrow, shan't I? You hadn't forgotten the course?'

'No, I hadn't forgotten. Are we travelling together? It would make sense to use one car, and mine is likely to still be at the garage. They phoned to say there were things that needed fixing.'

He nodded. 'You're right, it would make sense, and I was going to suggest it—but I promised Rachel I'd drop by her house at lunchtime, since it's on the way. Would you mind that? I could phone and let her know you'll be coming with me. I've some books she wanted to see— some information about Hodgkin's disease.'

Becky absorbed that with a sense of shock, her heart twisting painfully, not just for herself but because this must be hurting him so much, having to stand back and watch Rachel going through her living nightmare. She swallowed, forcing down the lump in her throat. 'I don't mind doing that, as long as it's all right with Rachel. I want to thank her for lending me the boots, anyway.' She paused, then asked carefully, 'Is it wise to take the medical books? Won't she be upset?'

'I don't think so, knowing Rachel. She probably feels she'll be able to cope better when she's more informed about what's happening.'

He dropped her off at the house a few minutes later, driving away with a curt nod that made her feel more rejected than ever. Yet she could understand how he must be feeling, and it had been her own fault that she'd let her guard down. It was too late now to tell herself that

she should have steered clear of Matthew, that she
shouldn't have let him get under her skin. It was much
too late for that. She was in love with him.

She phoned Drew that evening and told him it was all
over between them. It was a difficult conversation
because, as before, he didn't want to accept it.

'I'll come to the house,' he said. 'We can sort this out.'

'No. There's nothing left to say. I'm sorry, Drew. I
didn't mean to hurt you, but it just won't work for us.
We're not right for each other.'

Matthew was waiting for her after morning surgery had
finished the next day, and they set off in the lunchtime
traffic, heading for the other side of town, where Rachel
lived in a quiet suburb. Becky was subdued, her thoughts
going inward as she tried to steel herself for this meeting.
Jealousy was a horrible thing. She'd never experienced
it before, and she wasn't sure how she was going to
deal with it.

The front of the house was covered with neatly
trimmed ivy, and there was a roofed porch that still held
sparkling traces of frost. Rachel met them at the front
door and showed them into the house, going into
Matthew's embrace as though he was her lifeline.
Straightening a few moments later, she recovered herself,
and gave Becky a detached smile. With an effort, Becky
returned it, eyeing her rival with unwilling curiosity. She
was a slim woman, around the same age as Matthew,
with fine dark hair and gentle-looking grey eyes.

'I'm glad to meet you, Becky,' she greeted her as they
started along the hall. 'I hope you didn't mind being
dragged over here, but Matthew said it was on the way,
and he has some computer games for my son, Joel, as
well as the books for me. Joel will be really annoyed
when he finds that Matthew's come over here and he's
not been at home. Especially since Samantha's at home

today. There's a problem with the plumbing at her school.'

A young girl about nine years old appeared from another room. She smiled shyly at Becky but then forgot her self consciousness, running up to Matthew and throwing her arms around him.

'My bike's broken,' she told him dramatically. 'I fell off it and it's all twisted now, and Mummy says she can't mend it. Will you fix it for me?'

He lifted her in a bear hug. 'I'll do my very best,' he agreed. 'Where is it? Out in the back garden?'

He would have gone with her right away, but before Samantha could drag him off Rachel intervened.

'Lunch first,' she said firmly, pushing open a door and ushering them into the dining room. 'Come on in. I've laid a salad out in there; just help yourselves while I go and put the kettle on.'

Becky was about to offer to give her a hand, but something told her that Rachel wanted to be alone for a moment, and she subsided, letting the thought go. Matthew must have seen it too, because his expression was grim before he turned to look about the room. Becky saw that food had been set out on a sideboard, along with plates and cutlery, and an oval table had been laid with a white lace cloth, with cups and saucers positioned ready.

They went over to it, and Matthew offered her a plate then began to fill his own and Samantha's, helping the young girl to an extra serving of rice.

'You need building up,' he told her. 'You're too skinny. Turn you sideways and you'd be lost in a beam of sunlight.'

Samantha pulled a face, then laughed. 'Mummy says you could eat all day and you'd never put any weight on. I wish I was like that. I want to be a model when I grow up and wear all those glamorous clothes. Do you think I'll be tall enough, Matthew? Joel's bigger than me, but he's eleven.'

'I think you'll be crazy even to consider it,' he told her with a lift of his brows. 'Who wants to live on lettuce leaves for the rest of their working lives and end up looking like a walking skeleton?'

Becky listened to their banter and let her glance go around the room. A vase of flowers stood on the deep window-sill, catching the sunlight as it poured into the room. It was a homely place, finished with warm colours and soft furnishings, and there was a warm, cosy atmosphere that gave Becky a real pang. Seeing Matthew with Rachel had been bad enough, but watching him with Samantha had made her heart twist painfully. She could imagine him with children of his own, he'd make a good father, she was sure of it.

Across the room there was a cabinet with open-fronted shelves housing a collection of family photographs interspersed with ornaments. She recognised Rachel, and the man with her must have been her husband. It was a family picture and it had probably been taken some years ago because the boy, already showing signs of growing tall, looked only to be about six years old. There was a little girl who must have been Samantha, because the likeness, even all those years ago, was strong, but there was another child too in the picture—a little girl just a bit younger than Joel.

Rachel came in with the tea then and Matthew glanced at her soberly, quietly reading her expression.

'You must eat something too,' he said, when she would have ignored the food, and his gentle persistence gradually won through. She ate a little of what he put in front of her, and they talked about Steve, in hospital, though they were careful not to say anything that would alarm Samantha.

'It's early days, and he has several more chemotherapy sessions to go through,' Rachel said later, when Matthew went out to the back garden with Samantha to look at the bike and Becky was helping to clear the table. 'They say he has an eighty-five per cent chance of recovery. It's terribly hard just living each day as it comes.'

'It must be,' Becky murmured. 'But the treatment does work—he has a good chance of coming out of this with a complete recovery. It must be difficult for you, having to put on a front for the children, but I suppose at least it keeps you going. If there's anything I can do—'

'Thanks. People have been very kind, but I don't know what I'd have done without Matthew's support. He's been so good to me. And, of course, it helps, with him being a doctor; he's been able to answer my questions.'

'You've known each other a long time, haven't you?' Becky said, carrying dishes through to the kitchen.

'We practically grew up together.' Rachel piled plates into the dishwasher. 'Of course, we missed each other when he was away doing his medical training, but we kept in touch. It was always on the cards that he would go away. Matthew was always very clear about what he wanted to do.'

'Are his parents in the medical profession?' Becky asked.

'His grandparents are. They were both doctors, but they're retired now. His father's a physics lecturer and his mother's a pharmacist.' She closed the door on the dishwasher and set the programme. 'Matthew wanted to work with people. He always said he wanted to be there at the front line, so I suppose he always had it in mind to be a GP. I think he must be a good doctor, he's very committed to his work, always reading the latest research.'

'That's true enough,' Becky said. 'I know how determined he is to keep up to date and he's very thorough in everything he does. The patients love him.'

'Work always comes first with Matthew. I worry sometimes that he's too intense about it. He drives himself hard and he won't allow for any mistakes. He says you can't, not when you're dealing with people's lives every day.' Rachel frowned, occupied with her own thoughts for a moment, then she said, 'I'm sure that's part of the reason he's never settled down. Any relationship would always take second place to his work.'

She looked embarrassed suddenly, as though she might have said too much, and Becky wondered if she was thinking of another reason why there was no room for anyone special in his life. She made no comment, though, and just then Matthew came into the kitchen and went over to the sink to wash his hands.

'That's the bike fixed,' he said. He glanced at Rachel as she handed him a towel, and he seemed about to say something, but then his jaw clamped, and he turned to Becky instead. 'I think we'd better get on our way. We don't want to be late for the lecture.'

They left a few minutes later, thanking Rachel for the lunch and leaving Samantha to ride her bike round the garden. Becky wasn't sorry to be going. She'd found that she liked Rachel and that made things all the more difficult for her, understanding as she did what Matthew must have felt for her, what he perhaps still felt. She could see how he must be torn emotionally, and that made it so much harder to bear.

He was silent in the car, preoccupied, concentrating on the road ahead. They took their seats for the lecture in good time, and for the next four hours she was busy taking notes, watching a video, listening intently to what was going on. It made a change from being back at the health centre. It was good to be in different surroundings for once, to feel her mind being stretched, but most of all she was glad of Matthew's quiet presence beside her.

At the end of the session, they joined the crowd of people leaving the hall, and made their way out of the hospital. She paused while her eyes adjusted to the dark-

ness of the evening, and Matthew took her arm, steering
her towards the car park.

'That was a talk to give us food for thought,' he
remarked.

'Hmm. I'm a bit sceptical about some of the figures
they put out. I think they could have been interpreted in
several ways.'

Matthew laughed. 'Are you saying the professor was
biased?'

'Blinkered is the word I'd use.'

They were still arguing in a good-natured fashion as
they reached the car. The night had been closing in for
some time now and the darkness lent an added intimacy
to the dim interior of the car. She fastened the seat belt,
her fingers colliding with his, and the contact sent a surge
of heat along her limbs, and caused the breath to strangle
in her throat. Matthew went to switch on the ignition,
then paused, his glance meeting hers. He was so close
to her that she had only to move a fraction and her cheek
would graze his, her mouth might slide over the firm
angle of his jaw. Just thinking about it brought a rippling
warmth to suffuse her skin, and she felt her lungs
constrict.

'Becky,' he murmured huskily. 'Lord, Becky, do you
know what you do to me whenever you're near? Can
you begin to imagine how much I want to hold you?'
He took her hand in his and dragged it to his chest, so
that she felt the heat coming from him, and her skin
burned as though he'd lit a fuse. Beneath her fingers, his
heart pounded. 'Can you feel what you do to me?'

'I feel it,' she whispered. 'I want you too, Matthew,
but. . .' Perhaps it was being so near the hospital that
made her pause. She couldn't rid herself of the thought
that somewhere there, in one of the wards, Rachel's husband was lying ill. Had Matthew thought of that too?
Was he trying to blot out the past?

'Let's go home,' he muttered thickly. 'We've wasted

so much time.' Then he frowned as he saw the darkening of her eyes. 'What's wrong?'

'I'm not going to fall into bed with you,' she said shakily.

'You just said—'

'I know, but we need to talk; there are things we need to sort out.'

He stiffened and was silent for a moment, staring at her blankly as though she'd said something bizarre. Then she felt him move beside her, straightening as he put the car into gear and gunned the engine, taking them away from the hospital. Until then she hadn't realised that she had been holding her breath, but now as she eased herself back into her seat a soft sigh escaped her. Would there ever be a right time and place for them?

She didn't know how long they had been driving, and perhaps she'd been daydreaming, because it came on her with a faint sense of surprise that Matthew was slowing down the car, pulling up in the forecourt of an old coaching inn.

'Are we stopping here?' she asked, looking around, peering through the gloom at the sloping thatched roof and the white-painted front.

'I thought we might,' Matthew said. 'Neutral ground. That's what you wanted, wasn't it? Somewhere we can be alone without Sophie to interrupt us, and away from my flat where I might be tempted to leap on you.' His smile was cynical. 'I've been here once or twice before, I think you'll like it.'

They walked into the lounge bar. It was still fairly early and there were few customers as yet. Matthew left her seated in a quiet corner while he went to order drinks, and Becky looked around while she waited for him, taking in the polished brasses that hung on the walls and the cheerful little toby jugs that adorned the shelves. There was an inglenook fireplace where flames leapt upwards, adding a cheerful glow to the room, and a copper kettle gleamed in the hearth alongside a toasting fork. She smiled at the homely image then turned to glance at the other occupants of the room.

Two men stood at the bar chatting to the landlord, and seated at one of the tables was a couple in their fifties, enjoying a quiet drink. There was only one other person, a young man, who'd been standing at the bar but moved over to a cigarette machine out in the passage.

Matthew came back with the drinks—a glass of wine for her and a shandy for himself.

'I'm on call later,' he said. 'I must keep a clear head.' He'd brought with him a plate of sandwiches, and he put them down now on the table and pushed them towards her. 'Help yourself.'

'You said you'd been here before,' Becky murmured. 'I suppose it's reasonably close to the hospital. Have you worked there?'

'Only for a short time. This is my brother's haunt. He's a pharmaceutical rep, and whenever he's back in town we go out together for an evening. Several of my family live around here still.'

'You won't see so much of them, will you, when you're settled in at your new practice?' She had tried to forget that he would be leaving, but it was impossible, it was always there in the background, a lurking threat to her happiness.

'That's true. There are bound to be drawbacks to the move.'

'You won't be here for Steve, or Rachel either, will you?'

He looked serious, withdrawn for a moment. 'No. But perhaps that's just as well. The way things are, I'm always there as a reminder of the past.'

She flinched, bending her head so that he wouldn't see her reaction. He would miss Rachel when he went away, but perhaps she was the real reason behind his decision to take up a partnership some distance away. He was making a clean break.

They talked of other things for a while—about his family and various cousins scattered with their offspring around the country, and of Christmas coming soon. Becky wasn't absolutely sure of her plans yet, but she and Sophie would probably be staying with Rebeccah, and visiting the grandparents. She gazed absently into the fire, thinking of past years, when the whole family had been together, when there had been a lot of fun and laughter.

Matthew drained the last of his drink, and she sensed the restlessness in him. 'This was a bad idea,' he said. 'It isn't working. I want to be alone with you. Shall we go?' His eyes glittered, and she saw the determination written there as he reached for her hand and drew her away from the table. They walked out into the night air.

Security lights flickered into operation as they walked out across the gravel, and Becky saw that the young man from the pub was there, just staring at the light oddly, as though transfixed.

Matthew put an arm around her shoulders. 'Let's go home,' he suggested, and she nodded but turned to look back at the young man once more. Matthew followed her gaze. 'What's wrong?'

'I'm not sure,' Becky murmured. 'I saw him earlier in the pub. He seemed all right then, but there's something peculiar about the way he's staring at that light, something strange about it.'

'I see what you mean.' They stayed where they were, neither of them wanting to intrude at first, but just a short while later the man dropped to the ground. His whole body was rigid, and then the convulsions started.

Becky didn't stop to think any longer. She ran over to him, kneeling down beside him on the hard ground. His jerking movements were so strong that she was almost knocked off balance as his arms and legs thrashed wildly about.

'Can you loosen his collar?' she asked as Matthew came down beside her. The man was breathing noisily, his teeth clenched.

'Yes. Let me deal with him, you're liable to get hurt, the way he's flailing.' He tossed her a bunch of keys. 'There's a blanket in the boot of my car. Will you fetch it?'

She ran quickly to where he'd parked, struggling to find the right key and open the boot.

When she went back to Matthew, he was wiping the man's mouth, and she knelt down alongside him. The convulsions had stopped now, and between them they moved him into the recovery position and waited until he showed signs of regaining consciousness.

Becky covered him with the blanket, and watched him open his eyes and blink drowsily. After a while, he put a hand to his head, rubbing his temples and staring about him in confusion, looking bewilderedly from Matthew to Becky.

'Can you tell us your name?' Matthew asked.

'Harry,' the man said carefully, as though testing the sound of it on his tongue. He was frowning. 'Harry Fisher.'

'I'm a doctor,' Matthew said, 'and Becky here is a nurse. You're quite safe, there's nothing to worry about. We'll take care of you.'

'I don't know what happened.'

'I think you've had an epileptic fit,' Matthew told him. 'Have you had an attack before?'

'Once.' He rubbed his temples with his fingers. 'My head hurts.'

'You'll probably have a headache for a while, I'm afraid. One of the after effects of the fit. And there's a bump on your head where you banged yourself as you fell. I don't think it's anything serious but we ought to look at it in the light.'

'There was a light—' He broke off. 'I don't remember.'

'I think we should get you home,' Matthew said quietly. 'Can you tell us where you live? Is it far from here?'

Harry looked around, his expression vague.

'We're at a coaching inn,' Matthew said. 'You bought cigarettes earlier. Were you driving? Do you have a car here?'

'I don't remember. . . No. . .no. . .I walked. That's it, I walked. I live on Thorpe Crescent.'

'We'll take you there,' Matthew said. 'I've got my car. Can you stand?' He helped him find his feet as Becky tried to drape the blanket around him.

'Oh, Lord,' Harry said, a sick note in his voice. 'I'm soaking; I'm wet.'

'Don't worry about that,' Becky told him. 'It happens. We'll soon have you cleaned up.' She tucked the blanket round him more firmly and between them they helped him to Matthew's car.

Harry's parents were at home and they were shocked when they saw the state he was in.

'Is he on any medication?' Matthew asked, when Harry had gone upstairs to the bathroom with his father, but Mrs Fisher shook her head.

'When it happened before, they didn't say anything about giving him tablets or anything.'

'Well, I think now that he's had this second attack he should go back to his doctor,' Matthew said. 'He's probably going to need some kind of medication but your own doctor will be able to advise you.'

It was some half an hour later when they went back to the car, both of them quiet, the earlier mood gone. Matthew's phone bleeped as he slid behind the wheel, and he suppressed a sigh as he answered it. 'Work,' he said briefly, in answer to her unspoken query. 'I'll take you home.'

'Will I see you tomorrow?'

He shook his head. 'I have to go over to the new practice again.'

Becky was subdued and neither of them said much on the journey. She felt drained, empty, as though her emotions had gone through a wringer. So much seemed to have happened lately; everything seemed to have been turned upside down. Tonight, seeing that man lying helpless on the ground had somehow brought it home to her once again just how vulnerable people were.

Right now she felt that she was no exception. She had loved her parents but she had lost them, and now, when Matthew had come to mean so much to her, she was on the brink of losing him too. Already he was thinking ahead to his move down south. He would be going away in only a few short weeks and it wasn't very likely he would be looking back.

CHAPTER EIGHT

MATTHEW was away all that weekend, visiting the new practice, and the time dragged interminably for her. She filled her time by putting the finishing touches to the decorating, adding new curtains and cushions, but when the doorbell rang unexpectedly on Sunday afternoon her heart thumped and she went eagerly to answer it.

It wasn't Matthew, though. It was Drew, and her bubble of joy burst, though she made an effort not to let her dismay show.

'I hoped I'd find you here, alone. Aren't you going to invite me in?'

'I'm not alone. Sophie's here.' She bit her lip. 'Drew, I've tried to tell you—it's over between us. It won't work.'

His mouth made a bitter twist. 'We got on all right before. There's someone else, isn't there? That new doctor at the centre.'

'He wasn't the reason. You and I were growing apart before he came along. . . Perhaps I was never really sure of my feelings for you, but I know now that it wouldn't work. I'm sorry—but you have to accept it. It's over. Finished.'

He half turned, as though he was going to leave, but then he swung back to her and said, 'I don't want to let you go.' He moved closer, and before she'd realised his intention his arms came around her and he kissed her hard on the mouth. She was stunned by his action, unable to move or react in any way until he stepped back, releasing her.

'I'm sorry, Drew,' she said, and it was his turn to be shocked into silence. He swivelled away from her, and as she watched him walk back along the path she became aware of Matthew standing by his car, his expression frozen, a hard, grim mask. Then he jerked open the door, climbed in, and accelerated away, leaving a cloud of exhaust fumes to pollute the air.

She wished he hadn't seen that. What must he be thinking? But she could tell him what had happened, couldn't she? Next time they were together. . .

Back at the centre, though, she didn't get the chance to explain. In the odd moments when there was a lull between patients, there was always someone else around, or he was called away to deal with various crises that cropped up, and the mere fact of being so near him and yet so far away had her so wound up that the tension was beginning to scream along her nerve endings.

The clinics were busy in the run up to Christmas, and she was glad about that in a way because it left her with less time to think about things. Perhaps, after all, it was just as well that events had taken the turn they had. Matthew wasn't looking for marriage or commitment. His feelings were still bound up with Rachel and her family, and it was her own fault if she'd slowly been building up her hopes. He'd turned to her simply because she was there, because the woman he really wanted wasn't available. She wasn't going to be used as a substitute lover.

She closed her mind on her unhappy thoughts and turned her attention back to her waiting patients. This particular Friday afternoon had dragged on, and the last thing she needed was to be wallowing in self-pity.

'That looks as though it's healed up nicely, Mrs Davenport,' she said, inspecting some of Nick's handiwork a few minutes later. She consulted the notes on her screen. 'You had a small raised area of skin tissue removed, just over a week ago—is that right?'

Mrs Davenport nodded. 'Dr Tyler seemed to think it

was slightly out of the ordinary. I wasn't certain what it was, and you hear so much these days about being in the sun too long. We'd been away, you see. Somewhere hot, we thought, to get away from the English climate.'

'Have you been given the results of the biopsy?'

Mrs Davenport grimaced, biting on her lip. 'I was going to ask you about them rather than make a separate appointment to see the doctor.'

Becky consulted the notes once more, then gave the woman a smile. 'Everything's fine,' she said. 'It was clear; nothing to worry about at all.'

Relief showed in the woman's expression. 'That's good news,' she said.

'It is, isn't it? Dr Tyler made a very neat job of the stitches. They're ready to come out now—it shouldn't take above a minute or two.' Deftly, she dealt with the sutures and made a note on the records. 'All done.'

Her patient smiled, and put on her coat. 'I was really afraid it might be something nasty, but I can relax again now.'

'Of course you can,' Becky said, seeing her to the door.

Her last customer for the day was a young man in his early thirties, who limped into her room, his mouth contorted with pain. Helping him to a chair, she asked, 'What on earth have you been doing to yourself?'

'I twisted my foot, playing football. I'm not quite sure how I did it, but I dived for the ball and my foot went the other way. Dr Kingston's given me some anti-inflammatory tablets but he said I could have a support bandage on it as well, if I wanted.'

'No more football for a while, then, by the looks of things.' Becky eased the shoe from his foot, then the sock, and began carefully to bandage the ankle. 'Have you brought someone with you who can drive you home?' she asked him, and he nodded.

'My wife's waiting outside with the car. I expect she'll be ferrying me about quite a bit for the next week or so.'

Becky smiled at him. 'It's not long to Christmas, but it shouldn't interfere too much with that if you take care of it in the meantime.' When she finished with the bandage, she eased the sock on again. 'I'm not sure that we can get the shoe back on,' she said. 'Have you something looser back home that you can wear?'

'I'll sort something out.'

She helped him from the room and almost bumped into Matthew. The sight of him had her heart making a strange twist in her chest, sent a pulse to throb at the base of her throat. He always seemed to have this effect on her but she made a determined effort to fight the unsettling response. His expression was shuttered, and somehow she was wary of what his reaction might be if she took the time now to explain things. Anyway, if he cared anything for her, wouldn't he ask?

'Did you want me for something?' she murmured as he went with her into the treatment room.

'I just wanted to know if you could do a quick urine test for me,' he said. 'I suspect the patient's diabetic and we may need to do a blood test early next week.'

'Of course. I'll do it now.' She checked the specimen and showed him the test result a few moments later. 'It looks as though we'll have to fit a blood test in. There's a lot of sugar in there.'

Matthew grimaced. 'Will you make the appointment for her? She'll need a phone call to confirm it.'

She nodded, starting to clear things away. 'I'll see to it before I leave.' She turned away, but he caught hold of her arm. 'Charlotte's christening is this weekend,' he said. 'Your car's off the road again, isn't it? Martyn mentioned it to me. I could pick you up, and we can go to the church together.'

'That sounds a reasonable idea. I'm having a couple of tyres fitted. You have to drive past my place anyway, don't you?' She was busy tidying her cupboards in readiness for Monday's clinic, and she didn't trust herself to

do more than glance at him briefly, going on with what
she'd been doing.

'Will Sophie be coming along too?'

She shook her head. 'It's her birthday a few days after,
and her friends have arranged a trip out.'

On Sunday, the day of the christening, the sky was clear
and the sun shone with a bright energy that rapidly
cleared the crystalline frost and left everything looking
fresh and clean. Martyn and Sarah would be pleased, and
she felt glad for them.

She was almost ready, just putting the finishing
touches to her make up, when the doorbell sounded.

'I'll get it,' Sophie called.

Hearing Matthew's voice in the hall, Becky hastily
checked her reflection in the mirror. She felt the tension
rising inside her, knotting her muscles, and she made an
effort to be calm as she made her way downstairs. At
least she could feel fairly confident that she looked all
right. She was pleased with the fit of the new suit she'd
bought. Its lines were attractive, the jacket nipping in at
the waist and the skirt gently following the smooth curve
of hip and thigh. The back vent gave her ease of movement and on balance she was glad she'd chosen the soft
rose hue. It lent colour to her cheeks and complemented
the burnished silk of her hair.

Her lungs contracted in a sharp spasm as she saw him
standing there, looking incredibly handsome, immacu-
lately dressed in a dark suit and crisp linen shirt. His
glance moved over her, a glint of something unreadable
flickering in his green eyes.

'I'll be with you in a moment,' she told him huskily.
'I'll just go and collect my bag from the living room.'

He nodded briefly before turning back to Sophie.
Becky disappeared into the living room, but she heard
them chatting as she went to find her bag. With Sophie
he was gentle, his tone light.

'How are you these days?' he was asking. 'Are you looking after yourself properly? No more hiccups with the treatment?'

'I'm doing OK,' Sophie answered.

'It won't be long now until the end of term,' Matthew said. 'Are you looking forward to the Christmas holiday?'

'I'm looking forward more to leaving school all together,' Sophie told him bluntly. 'By the time next summer comes I want to be independent, earning my own money.'

'I thought you were staying on?' Matthew's brow lifted a fraction.

'What's the point in studying for years when I can just as easily get a job in an office and start making a living for myself?'

Coming back into the hall, Becky halted abruptly in the doorway. 'And what skills do you have for working in an office?' she asked.

'I'll learn to type,' Sophie told her. 'When Drew phoned the other day, he said he'd let me have a typing programme. I could teach myself on the word processor upstairs.'

Matthew frowned. 'Why would he encourage you to do something like that?'

Sophie flicked him a sideways glance. 'He was being sweet to me,' she said. 'What other reason would he have?'

Becky was having trouble containing the shock. Hadn't she made it clear enough to Drew that they had no future together? Why was he still intent on interfering? What did it take to get him to accept the situation? But perhaps this was a simple act of revenge, as she suspected the kiss had been last Sunday afternoon. He must have known that Matthew was watching.

'You're not serious?' she said now. 'About the typing, I mean? You had the chance to do that at school, last year, and you turned it down. You didn't want to work in an office.'

'So, I changed my mind. There's nothing wrong with that, is there?'

Becky shook her head in a bewildered fashion. 'But. . . this notion of leaving school. . .I thought it was just a passing phase—you can't give up, not now. You're intelligent, you're an artist, you're creative. Don't you think you should do something with that talent?'

'I told you, I don't want years of studying. OK, so I can draw passably well, but where's that going to get me?' She stared at Becky defiantly. 'I know all the arguments. I've heard them all before and I haven't got time to go through them all again. I've got to go, or I shall be late.'

Matthew halted her with a hand on her arm as she would have turned away. 'Before you go, Sophie—I bought something for you.' He picked up a small package from the hall table and handed it to her. 'Becky told me it was your birthday soon.'

Becky watched Sophie's wondering expression and felt something twist in her chest. She might have known Matthew would do something like this.

Sophie turned the parcel over in her hand. 'You bought this for me?' she said, a note of surprise in her voice.

'Open it, if you want,' he said, with a smile, seeing the excitement in her expression. 'Unless you'd rather wait. . .'

The temptation was too much for Sophie, though, and she tugged at the wrapping paper, still with a look of surprised pleasure in her eyes. It was a book about oil-painting techniques, with a scooped-out place for small tubes of colour and pages for sketching at the back of the book. She ran her fingers over it and looked up at him, smiling.

'It's great, thanks.'

'I saw it when I was in town and I thought you might

like it,' he murmured. 'Some of your sketches showed real promise, I thought. Even if you don't intend to take it up on a major scale, it's a good pastime.'

'That was very thoughtful of you,' Sophie told him, her mouth moving a little uncertainly. 'Thanks, Matthew.' Then, glancing at the clock on the wall, she added hurriedly, 'Yipes, I'm really late. I must go.' She headed towards the front door, calling back to Becky as she went, 'Remember, I'm at Stacey's tonight—see you later.'

She left the house and Becky stared after her, shaking her head. 'I didn't want to argue with her, but some time soon we're going to have to sit down together and have a proper talk. She's a bright girl, but she seems to be determined on wasting her life and ignoring good advice. It isn't just me—her teachers have advised her to stay on, yet she's fighting all the way. I just don't know how to get through to her. She's never been like this before, so uptight and obstinate. I don't understand what's got into her. I know there's been a lot of unhappiness and uncertainty in her life, but I thought moving here would be a good thing, a solid base to work from, providing some security in her life from here on.'

His lips compressed. 'It seems to me that it's Drew you should be talking to. From the sound of things, he's doing a first-rate job of undermining everything you're trying to achieve, but perhaps you're too blind to see it.'

'You know so much, do you, about my relationship with him?'

'Enough to know that he isn't right for you. I've heard him talk, I've seen you with him, and I get the strong impression that your feelings come second to anything else as far as he's concerned. He only looks at life from his point of view, and I doubt very much that he's the kind of man who will ever change. If you took the time to stop and think about it, you might see that you two aren't in the least bit suited.'

He was a fine one to talk, wasn't he, carrying a torch for a married woman? 'And aren't you another one who thinks he knows best?' she retorted hotly. 'Who are you to tell me what I should do, when your own life is in a state of constant upheaval? You told me yourself that you're always on the move, you've never settled anywhere for long, and aren't you doing the same thing now—running away?'

'That's the most crack-brained statement I've ever heard. My career is important to me—'

'So much that you're prepared to leave your family and friends behind?'

His mouth twisted at that. 'Aren't we getting away from the point? My motivation wasn't the topic under discussion. It's Sophie's future that's in jeopardy, not mine, and anyway, she won't be able to make a decision about that until the spring, so there's no immediate need for concern. And we don't have time to go into it right now.' He checked his watch. 'We should be getting a move on, or we'll be late.'

Becky nodded distantly and went with him to the door, suppressing a sigh. He was right, this wasn't the moment to be thinking about it, and it was her problem, not Matthew's. He was a bachelor—footloose and fancy-free; why should he want to get involved with the difficulties of dealing with a teenage girl?

They arrived at the church in time to take their seats for the service, and she tried to put everything from her mind and concentrate on what was going on. Already in an emotionally charged state, she felt a lump in her throat as Sarah held the baby in her arms by the font. Five-year-old Daniel, a little awestruck by the proceedings, stood beside her, looking unusually spruce in a smart grey suit, and Becky was struck by the likeness between mother and son, both with their bright fair hair and the delicate line of nose and mouth.

Martyn held Daniel's hand throughout the service,

only letting him go when they moved outside into the bright, cold sunshine. Then Daniel whooped along the path to the waiting car, scuffing up the fallen leaves with his shoes as he went. Becky watched him, a wistful smile curving her mouth.

Martyn and Sarah's house was warm and welcoming when they all arrived back there about an hour later. A mouth-watering buffet had been set out in the large kitchen, and people helped themselves to delicious vol-au-vents and triangular cut sandwiches. Becky, aware of Matthew standing at her side, felt oddly isolated from the buzz of laughter and chatter all around her, until Daniel came up to the table and gave her a wide smile, and she found herself returning it.

Martyn's mother helped him to pastries and crisps and he stuffed them into his mouth as though he hadn't eaten for several hours. He caught Becky's amused glance and announced, 'Becky lives in my house, you know, Nan. The one where Mummy used to live. Do you think she'll have a baby next?'

Matthew choked suddenly, muffling the sound behind his hand, and Becky, disguising a grin, said soberly, 'I shouldn't think that'll happen for quite a while, Daniel. You'll have to make do with your sister for the time being.'

He shrugged at that. 'She's all right, for a girl, but I wanted Mummy to have a boy.' He took another handful of crisps. 'I might let her play with my cars, though, when she's bigger. So long as she doesn't break them.' Yet another crisp went into his mouth.

His mother walked into the room, handing round glasses of wine. 'She's going to be a tomboy,' she said. 'I can feel it in my bones. Even now she follows his every move.'

Becky and Matthew accepted a glass from her. 'Martyn tells me you were asking him the other day about some notes he has on countryside walks,' Sarah said, addressing Matthew. 'He had them bound into a couple of small volumes—they're in the study if you and Becky want to take a look at them.'

'Thanks. It's my turn to organise the next one,' he murmured, shooting a glance at Becky. 'Shall we?'

Becky nodded.

'Are you going along on that one?' Sarah asked, watching her expectantly.

'Maybe.' She wasn't altogether sure it would be such a good idea to spend another day with him, but the mere suggestion had her heart thumping, and if he asked again she doubted she'd have the will-power to turn down his invitation.

They followed Sarah to the study. 'There are a few books on places to visit within a sixty-mile or so radius,' she told them, going over to a bookcase and pulling out a few leather bound volumes which she transferred to a polished table. 'You might like to browse through those as well. Feel free to borrow them if you like.'

All three of them glanced through the books for a while, commenting on the beautiful photography and careful illustrations, until Sarah said on a note of apology, 'I'll leave you to it, if you don't mind. I left Charlotte with Jessica, and I ought to go and check that she's all right. Nick was still filling his plate up last time I looked, and she might need some support.'

Becky sent Matthew a puzzled glance as Sarah left the room. 'What was that about?' she asked quietly. 'Nick's wife's a health visitor, isn't she? I'd have thought she'd be the last person to need support.'

'True,' Matthew agreed. 'From what I've gathered so far, she manages very well, but this is probably an especially emotional time for her. They would like a family of their own, but Jessica's had problems in the past and it may not happen. They just have to wait and see, I suppose.'

Becky felt her heart twist in sympathy for Jessica. 'We

take so much for granted, don't we?' she murmured. 'We tend to assume that marriage and families automatically go together.'

'I suppose most women do. It's a more natural commitment for them.'

'You sound as though you have doubts.' Becky studied him, uncertainty etching a line into her brow.

'I think I do,' he admitted frankly. 'I'm not so sure that I'd want a family. I don't know how I'd cope if a child of mine became very ill, if I'd given it years of love and then it was snatched from me. I think of myself as a strong person but I don't know if I could handle that. I've seen it happen and I know how much pain it brings.'

She understood what he was saying but still his words brought an unwelcome surge of anxiety to twist her stomach into knots. 'You see it because you're a doctor,' she began hesitantly. 'You see the cases that are brought in—tragic cases sometimes—but they're only a small portion of the population. You can't think so negatively, you can't wait for something bad to happen.'

'I know that,' he said, 'but I've been too close to it. I've seen it happen to people I care about. I know the heartache it can cause and I wouldn't ever want to go through that.'

Becky's gaze flickered uncertainly as she thought back over all he'd told her about his family, about his parents and his grandparents, but she was sure there'd been no mention of any tragedy. Perhaps she was treading on thin ice here, but even so she was prompted to say quietly, 'Can you tell me about it? What happened?'

He shook his head. 'No, I don't think I can. Not here, not now. I don't want to dwell on what happened in the past. It's over, finished, and I'd rather forget.'

She shouldn't have asked, but nevertheless, the rejection hurt and her mouth wavered a fraction. Had this something to do with Rachel? She remembered the day they'd visited, and she thought of the photographs she'd seen. Instinct told her there was a connection, and her heart twisted painfully.

'Couldn't I help some way? Just by listening?' She touched his arm in a gesture of understanding, and he looked at her, his expression serious.

'Don't expect more of me than I can give, Becky.'

'I've never asked anything of you.'

'No,' Matthew answered, 'you haven't, and in a way that makes it worse. You're a sweet girl.'

He turned his head as though he would have returned to looking at the books once more, but she had seen the bleakness in his eyes, and she wrapped her arms about him, laying her cheek against the linen of his shirt.

'Don't shut me out, Matthew. . .please?'

She felt the sudden tensing of his muscles, heard the slow release of his breath, before his palm cradled the back of her head and his fingers tangled with the silk of her hair.

His lips brushed her forehead and she tilted her face up to him, searching his expression. There was stark need etched in his green eyes, and after the first faint sense of shock ebbed away her mouth softened, her lips parting in subtle invitation.

'Ah, Becky,' he muttered thickly, and in the next instant he was claiming her mouth with bruising passion, and easing her against his long body, his hands smoothing over her soft curves. He kissed her slowly, deeply, sparking a response that raged like fire through her body. Her fingers trembled as she explored the velvety hardness of his chest, the muscled strength of his arms, and slowly, as his mouth slid down over her throat and his ragged words of need were muffled against her skin, a tiny glow of hope flickered to life in her. He wanted her, and that was a start, surely? Maybe, one day, he would come to return her love in equal measure.

As the thought surfaced in her mind, his glance meshed

with hers, his eyes darkening with passion, and she felt the thud of his heartbeat quicken beneath her fingers. His hands slid over her, a little unsteady at first, then as he drew in a harsh breath his palm cupped her breast, his thumb moving caressingly over the hardening nub until a soft shudder of desire escaped her.

'I need you,' he said, his voice roughened. 'How have I managed to get by so long without you?' The clock chimed in the hall and his whispered murmurings turned to a low groan. Matthew stilled, listening to the chiming of the hour, then drew her head against his chest and stroked her hair, his thumb moving in circles at the nape of her neck.

'I always believed I could stay in complete control,' he muttered. 'I always knew where I was headed, what I was doing, until I met you, and now everything's shot to pieces.'

Becky whimpered faintly, her fingers curling against the taut muscles of his chest. 'Me too,' she whispered, then gave a low moan as the sound of footsteps in the hall filtered through. 'Someone's coming.'

He leaned his head against her cheek for a long moment, then slowly, with obvious reluctance, he put her away from him, and she straightened, her body aching with unfulfilled desire.

'Later?' he whispered. 'I have to go through some paperwork with Martyn later today—it's urgent, he says—but I could come to you at the house this evening. I need to talk to you, to be with you. Can we be alone? Just the two of us?'

She nodded, unable to trust her voice, and he smiled—a crooked, rueful smile that set her veins on fire and made her legs go weak. Somehow, just then, the evening seemed a long, long way off.

CHAPTER NINE

BACK at the house a few hours later, Becky added the finishing touches to the table she'd laid in readiness for Matthew's arrival. Candlelight and winter flowers, a bottle of wine in readiness alongside two long-stemmed glasses—had she thought of everything? But what if she'd read too much into his mood this afternoon? What if he'd changed his mind? Her stomach twisted in a spasm of jittery excitement. She wouldn't think that way. He'd said he wanted her, needed her, and that was what mattered, wasn't it?

She was humming quietly to herself, a soft smile pulling at the corners of her mouth, when the kitchen door opened and Sophie came into the room. Becky looked at her in surprise, noting the distracted way she threw her bag down onto a chair and the faint sigh that went along with the action.

'I thought you were going to spend the evening at Stacey's house—is everything all right?'

'Her auntie's had a fall and they've all had to rush over to her house to help out. Stacey's going to look after her cousins while her parents take the aunt to the hospital. I'd have gone with them, only they don't know how long they'll be away—they might need to stay overnight.'

'Oh dear, I'm sorry. Was it a bad fall?'

'An awkward one, I think. She slipped and did something to her wrist. It sounded as though it was painful, anyway.'

'Poor thing. So you're at a loose end, are you?' It was a shame that Sophie's plans had fallen through, but she was trying not to let that spoil her own anticipation of the evening ahead.

'Looks that way.' Sophie's glance went around the neat kitchen and settled on the carefully arranged table. 'Is Matthew coming over?'

Becky nodded, and went to check the savoury rice that was steaming gently on the hob. 'In about half an hour.'

'I thought you were looking cheerful when I walked in.' Sophie's sage expression was somehow much older than her years. 'Are you cooking something special?'

'Not exactly. I'm not altogether sure whether he'll have eaten or not, so I've done a mixture of hot and cold dishes, and a salad, so we can sit down to eat, or pick at bits and pieces as we feel like it. There should be enough for three, though,' Becky added, not missing Sophie's appreciative sniff. 'Are you hungry?' She turned the rice out into a serving dish as the phone rang, and Sophie went to answer it.

'Oh, hello, Matthew. . . No, something came up, and I had to give it a miss. . .'fraid so; I'll have to make do with TV here instead, I suppose. Did you want to talk to Becky?'

Becky looked across at her, and wiped her hands on a towel before going over there to take the receiver.

Had there been a glitch in their plans? She fought off the notion as she greeted him, but when he answered he didn't sound quite like his usual self, and the sinking feeling came back again, full force. There was an odd note to his voice, as though he was preoccupied with something, and she was prompted to ask, 'Is something wrong?'

She heard the grimace in his voice. 'I may not be able to make it tonight, after all. I'm sorry, Becky. It's just that Rachel phoned; she's in a bit of a state, and I have to go and see her. It's a bad time for her—'

'It's all right,' she cut in, fighting off the sudden wave of nausea that threatened to overwhelm her. Rachel only

had to call and he dropped everything to go to her. 'You
don't have to explain. I understand.' Her senses were
numbed, and when she spoke again her voice was cool,
distant. 'It wasn't important, after all, and I expect I'll
see you at the centre tomorrow, anyway.'

'I'm out in the morning, on call—'

'Whenever.' She didn't want to hear any more. 'It
doesn't matter. You do what you have to.'

She didn't want to prolong the call. Matthew had his
mind on other things, and there was nothing to be gained
by keeping him talking when he wanted to go to Rachel.
Tears stung her eyelids and she blinked them away.
Rachel was worried or upset, and that was understandable; she ought to be able to see his reasoning. . . Or
maybe it had simply been an excuse because he'd had a
change of heart. He'd had time, hadn't he, to think things
through, and to regret the afternoon? Either way, she
could do nothing to stop the feeling of despondency that
threatened to swamp her, and all the time she was conscious of Sophie watching her, of the need to put on a
brave front. She broke off the conversation, saying a
quick goodbye, and then went back to the hob, turning
off the gas.

'Looks like it's just going to be you and me, then,'
she said, in a matter-of-fact tone, relieved that her voice
didn't betray her. 'We'll have to polish this lot off
between us.' She pulled plates out of the warming grill
and set them down on the table.

'Isn't he coming?' Sophie frowned at the quick shake
of her head. 'Why not? Is he on call?'

'No.' It came out more stiffly than she'd intended.
'Something came up, and he has to go out. Will you put
the bread rolls out for me?' She busied herself with the
various dishes, until there was nothing more to do but
sit down at the table. 'Pity it's getting late, or we could
have gone to the cinema. Still, there's always a video.'

Sophie slid into her seat, glancing at her. 'I'm sorry,'

she said. 'You were looking forward to seeing him tonight, weren't you?'

Becky lifted her shoulders in a negative gesture. 'It can't be helped. I dare say there'll be other times.' She wasn't altogether sure that was true, but she didn't want to let the alternative surface and take form. Already there was a hollow place inside her, a void, where before there had been hope. He had gone to Rachel as soon as she'd called. Rachel. . .the woman he had loved. . .still loved?

Somehow, she managed to get through the rest of the evening, though she went up to bed earlier than usual, making an excuse to Sophie, feeling unaccountably tired. She buried herself under the duvet, and sleep came at last, dark and comforting, taking away the burden of the day.

She woke with a splitting headache, and went off to work alone, leaving Sophie at home since it was the start of her Christmas break.

'Will you be OK?' she asked, hesitating, her hand on the door. Sophie looked pale this morning, and she had been much quieter than usual, though perhaps she just needed a lie-in. 'I could come home at lunchtime, if you like.'

Sophie shook her head. 'No need. I'm meeting Louise later. We'll probably go shopping in town for some last-minute presents.'

Becky nodded, and left her to it. 'Ring me if you change your mind, or want to talk.'

She had a full clinic to deal with first thing, and after that she was scheduled to assist Nick Tyler with minor ops. There was hardly time to breathe, though at least it meant that the hours passed quickly. When she was finally through, though, and she found herself with a free half-hour, there was still no opportunity for her to see Matthew. He was shut in his room dealing with a steady stream of patients, and when her shift for the day finished he was in the middle of a meeting with a rep. There was no knowing how long that might take, so she drove home, schooling herself to put on a bright face for Sophie.

Only, Sophie wasn't home, which was odd, and within minutes of Becky's arrival Stacey phoned.

'I've been trying to reach her all day,' she said in frustration. 'Do you know where she might be?'

'With Louise?' Becky hazarded.

'No. Louise hasn't seen her either. None of the gang knows where she is. No one's seen her at all today.'

That was strange. More than that, it was downright worrying, because Sophie had never been known to break arrangements, and there was an unspoken agreement that she and Becky would always let each other know where they might be. After Stacey had rung off, Becky stood thinking things through for a moment. Could something be wrong? Was she ill somewhere and not able to get home?

Her mind flitted through all the alternatives, leaving her with a cold sensation of fear in the pit of her stomach. Maybe there was some simple explanation, though. She ought at least to check what Stacey had said before she started jumping to conclusions.

She phoned around, but the end result was the same lack of information. No one had had sight or sound of Sophie all day. Where on earth could she be?

The doorbell chimed just then, breaking into her thoughts, and she jerked a little, before she collected herself and hurried to answer it. Perhaps Sophie had forgotten her key.

It wasn't Sophie, though, but Matthew, and he looked at her quizzically as she simply stared at him.

'Can't I come in?'

She pulled the door wide, still abstracted, and he stepped inside, a frown tugging his dark brows together.

'Becky?' he said quietly, a note of concern in his voice. 'Has something happened? Tell me.' He pushed the door shut behind him, then touched her arm with his hand, so that she looked up into his face, absorbing the fact that he was here, at last, after she'd waited all day to see him. He was here, but that could mean anything. It could mean that he'd come to realise finally that he had no future with Rachel. . .or—

She cut off the thought. She ought to have been glad of his presence, but instead her mind was revolving in distracted circles and getting nowhere.

'I don't know where Sophie is,' she said unevenly. 'She hasn't been seen all day, and it isn't like her to go off like that, without leaving word. I'm worried about her, Matthew. What if she's been taken ill? I need to find her, but I don't know where to look.'

He took her in his arms and held her close, and that made things worse somehow. She wanted desperately to take refuge in the comfort he was offering, and for a moment her tears dampened his shirt until she dashed them away with the back of her hand. She had to be strong, to stand on her own two feet, because his nearness was just a temporary thing, and in a week or so he'd be on his way down south, to a new life. He was concerned for her, but she shouldn't read anything into that, because he was a caring man and he would show compassion for anyone who needed help.

'We'll find her, Becky. Don't get yourself all upset. Between us, we'll sort it out, you'll see. Didn't she give you any idea what she might be doing today?'

'She said she was going shopping. She was going with her friend, Louise, but Louise hasn't heard from her. She didn't turn up.'

'Perhaps she went on her own.'

She shook her head. 'I don't think she would do that.' Her fingers clenched until her nails dug into her palms and her knuckles went white. 'Besides, it's dark now. She'd have been back hours ago.'

'OK,' he said calmly, still holding her, his hands firmly about her shoulders, warm and strong. 'Let's think of the alternatives. Was anything troubling her? Did she seem all right this morning?' As he spoke, he led her towards the living room, his arm sliding around her, keeping her by him in a firm embrace.

'She was a bit quiet, I suppose,' she said, sniffing a little. 'I thought she was still tired, so I didn't question it. Maybe I should have—' She broke off, uncertainty creeping into her eyes, fresh tears stinging her eyelids. 'Perhaps it's this business of leaving school. . .'

'Don't, Becky. You can't live in her head, so stop blaming yourself. Try to think where she might go when she wants to be alone.'

She stared at him blankly. 'There's nowhere. . .only the country park, near where we used to live.' She shook her head again, making the chestnut curls fall untidily across her cheek. 'She wouldn't be there—not now, not with night coming on.'

'Why would she go there?'

'I don't know. It was just a wild guess; I'm clutching at straws, that's all. We used to walk there sometimes with Dad, in the summer. He and Sophie used to take the path up to a little stone shelter at the top of the hill, and he'd produce a flask of cold milk and some chocolate, and they'd wolf it down as though it was a real treat. I suppose it was, for Sophie.' Her voice trailed miserably. 'She'd had to be so careful about what she ate when her diabetes was first diagnosed and we were trying to get her diet sorted out.'

'We'll try there first, then. Leave a note for her, in case she comes back while we're out.'

He took over from then on, and it was a relief not to have to think, to make decisions on her own. She hurried to get her coat and push a few things into her bag, spurred into action by his cool command of the situation. They drove out into the countryside, following the bus route, in case they should come across her by chance, walking the lanes.

The gates that gave on to the west side of the deer park creaked open, allowing them access to the hill path, and they followed its winding course, their torch beams picking out the rough, stony ground. They found the shelter, and looked around, checking the walls and the corners with the light, but it was empty. Even though she hadn't really expected to find Sophie there, a wave of dejection washed over her, hunching her shoulders and making her shiver.

Matthew took her in his arms, hugging her to him. 'We will find her, Becky.' He pulled up her coat collar, kissing her lightly, his lips merely brushing hers but bringing them to tingling life. 'Try not to worry. Think for a minute. Is there anywhere else around here she liked to visit?'

She drew herself up and said flatly, 'There's an old hall, on the next rise. It's centuries old, just ruins, but we could give it a try.'

Matthew took her hand in his, his large fingers warmly enveloping her palm, and they headed across the heather-covered slopes until they reached the remains of the stone-walled building. They walked around the perimeter walls until Matthew's light picked out the arched entrance, and Becky said hoarsely, 'Listen, did you hear something? I thought—'

'I heard it too,' he said. 'Through here...'

They found Sophie huddled against the cold, in a flat, recessed arch that might once have been a store place. Becky put her arms around her and hugged her, rubbing warmth into her icy limbs.

'Sophie...what are you doing here? You're freezing,' she said brokenly. 'I've been so worried. I didn't know what had happened to you.'

Sophie stirred faintly, but her voice sounded far away and rough-edged, as though she was waking from a deep sleep, and Becky stared into her face anxiously, willing her to focus.

Matthew checked her over quickly, then slid a glucose tablet into her mouth. 'Come on, Sophie, try to stay with it,' he urged, pulling her into his arms and lifting her away from the damp ledge. 'We'll take you to the car and get you warmed up. Hold on. Put your arms round my neck.' He straightened, and Sophie made a muffled groan as though she was in pain.

'Are you hurt?' Becky asked, and struggled to catch the faint answer. She glanced at Matthew. 'I think she might have done something to her foot.'

He nodded. 'I'll take a proper look once we get home. For now, we'd best get her warm and keep her glucose up.'

He carried her out of the ruins and back to the path, his breath freezing on the cold air. Becky led the way to the car, wrenching open the door so that he could place her sister on the back seat and wrap a blanket snugly around her. Within minutes, he set the car in motion and they took the road for home. Becky's heart was thudding heavily, the tension of the day catching up with her, her mind filled with a myriad of questions that she couldn't voice.

She had never been so glad to see the welcoming light by her door as she was now when they drew up in front of the house. It signalled warmth and safety, and a return to sanity. Matthew lifted Sophie in his arms once more and carried her into the living room, and between them they coaxed her back to something near her usual self.

'That ankle's badly sprained,' Matthew said, after he had completed his examination. 'You'll need to rest it for some time. Here—take these.' He handed her a couple of painkilling tablets from his case and watched her swallow them with the hot tea Becky had made. 'Can you tell us what happened. . .what you were doing out there?'

'I wanted to be on my own for a while.' Sophie sipped at the tea, cupping the mug with her hands. 'I needed to think. I didn't mean to worry you, honestly, Becky. I was going to come home, but I hurt my ankle and I couldn't get away from the ruins, the pain was so bad. I thought I'd just rest it for a while, but I started to feel sleepy—it must have been all the walking that did it. Too much exercise, and not enough food. I'd taken some biscuits with me, but I finished all those this morning.'

Becky's fingers tightened on the folds of her skirt. 'Why didn't you talk to me if something was troubling you, instead of going off on your own like that? Why can't you tell me what's bothering you?'

'I needed to work things out for myself. I'm in the way, I know I am. I ruined it for you with Drew, and now the same's happening with Matthew, isn't it? I thought maybe I could leave home, get a job and support myself, but—'

Becky was horrified. 'You mustn't even begin to think like that. Of course you're not in the way. I'd already told Drew it wasn't working, and I didn't want to see him again. We would have parted company anyway; we just weren't right for each other. I realised that some time ago. He was too selfish, too full of his own needs to consider anyone else.'

She felt Matthew's glance home in on her, and she flushed slightly. Perhaps he was recalling that he'd told her so. She took a breath and went on, 'When he phoned you the other day, he was just trying to get at me, through you. I rang him yesterday and told him again that it was over. I think this time he well and truly got the message.'

Sophie gave a faint sigh. 'Do you mean that? I never really liked him. I don't think he liked me much, and I always had the feeling that I was in the way. But I tried to get on with him, Becky, for your sake. I was glad, at first, when he went off the scene, but then I felt guilty for feeling that way. I thought I might have driven you apart.'

'You mustn't blame yourself,' Becky said vehemently. 'Believe me, we just weren't suited.'

'But it's different with you and Matthew, isn't it?'

Sophie eyed her shrewdly. 'You're in love with him, I can tell, and you're right for each other. But it's happening all over again, isn't it? I'm in the way. I'll always be in the way.'

Becky shook her head vigorously. 'You're not in the way. You must never, ever think that.' She put her arms about her and hugged her close. 'You're my sister, and I think the world of you—'

'But it's true,' Sophie persisted, her voice rising a notch. 'You were so happy when you thought he was coming round here yesterday, and then he phoned and he knew that I'd be here, and that's why he didn't come. I know you said he had to go somewhere, but that was just an excuse he made, wasn't it? I'm spoiling things for you both.' She broke off, stifling a sob. 'I know it, I've known it all along, but I don't know what to do to make it different.'

Becky gasped, but before she could say anything Matthew put in quietly, 'That isn't how it was at all, Sophie. The thing is, a friend of mine, Rachel, was upset because her husband is very ill in hospital. She lost a child some years ago, and she was desperately afraid she was going to lose her husband too. I think, with it being so near to Christmas, she was thinking about her family and feeling really low. She asked me to go and see her, to talk to her, and I didn't think I could let her down when she needed me.'

He paused, and Becky touched his arm, her face pinched with sadness. 'She lost a child? The little girl in the photo? Oh, Matthew. . .'

'Her name was Maris,' he said. 'She was the sweetest thing, always lively, full of fun, mischievous.' He half turned, so as to include Sophie. 'I used to see the family a lot. Rachel had been my girlfriend at one time; we'd been engaged. Things hadn't worked out between us; we'd both realised we weren't right for each other, and after we'd called it a day we stayed friends. I introduced

her to Steve, and they clicked with each other straight
away. It was good to see them so happy together, and
when the children came along everything seemed just
perfect for them. Joel was only a year older than his little
sister, but he used to boss her around, get her into all
kinds of scrapes. They were inseparable. There was a
bond between them.' He stopped speaking, his mouth
compressing with pain.

'I was away at medical school,' he went on, 'when
she was taken ill. I didn't know anything about it until
much later. Rachel had tried to phone, but the message
didn't get through. One minute she'd been all right, but
within a few hours she was desperately sick. They took
her to hospital, but it was already too late. She had meningitis and in the space of just a few hours she was dead.
It was so difficult to take it in. I find it hard to forgive
myself that I wasn't there, that I wasn't able to do anything, that a tiny life can be gone in the blink of an eye.'

'Oh, Matthew, I'm so sorry,' Becky said. 'So very,
very sorry.' She saw the bleak emptiness in his eyes and
drew in a deep, shaky breath. 'You can't blame yourself,
you have nothing to blame yourself for.'

'I suppose I know that, deep down, and I've tried to
forget, but you can't, you know. It isn't possible.' His
shoulders moved slightly, his spine straightening. 'It was
a long time ago,' he said. 'But last night Rachel was
feeling really low, all the memories came flooding back
to her, and she needed to talk to me, and I felt I had to
help her through it as best I could.'

He looked at Sophie. 'Do you see how it was, Sophie?
I couldn't let her down when she turned to me, even
though I wanted more than anything to be with Becky.
I talked to Rachel, and I took her to the hospital to see
Steve and I tried to reassure her that he's on the mend.
That's all I can do, really—give them both my support.'

'Is he on the mend?' Becky sent him a troubled glance.

'I believe so. I spoke to the consultant last night, and

he said Steve was responding to treatment. I think Rachel had seen him at the end of his chemotherapy, when he was feeling grim, and that's what upset her more than anything and put doubts in her mind. She seemed happier after she'd talked to him and the consultant yesterday.'

'I'm glad.' Becky touched his arm lightly, her mouth curving in a faint smile.

'So. . .' Sophie looked unsure of herself. 'I was wrong, then—you and Becky aren't going to split up because of me?'

'I sincerely hope not,' Matthew said with a frown. 'I hope you were right when you said that Becky loves me.' He turned to Becky, taking her hands in his. 'Because that's all I need to know. Everything else we can work out between us, just as long as there's love.'

'Oh, yes,' Becky whispered, her heart squeezing tight in her chest as the enormity of what he was saying came home, and he looked down at her, his eyes gleaming warmly, his mouth moving in a bone-melting smile.

'Good. That's settled, then. Like I said before, aeons ago, we have a lot to talk about.' Glancing down at Sophie, he said with a wry grin, 'But we'll go and do that somewhere private, if you don't mind, young lady. I'm quite happy to have you around for the next umpteen years, but from time to time I shall grab Becky's undivided attention. Like right now. . .'

'But. . .' Sophie stopped him as he was about to grab Becky's hand. 'I thought you were going away. . . There's this job you're going to. . .'

His expression sobered. 'In the new year, yes. That's one of the things we have to talk about. I know Becky set a lot of store in staying here, in giving you a solid base, but I'm hoping I can persuade her to uproot everything once more. It'll mean a change of scene along with a change of job, and a different school or community college, or whatever, for you. I hope she won't mind that, that neither of you will have too many objections, otherwise I shall have to rethink my own career.' He turned questioningly towards Becky. 'You've established yourself in this job, I know, but—'

She shook her head. 'I can follow a nursing career anywhere. As to this place—it's people that matter, not bricks and mortar. I'll go wherever you go...if Sophie will come too.'

His mouth curved. He took her hand in his and gave it a gentle squeeze before turning back to Sophie. 'What do you think? It's still within commuting distance. I shall have to come back regularly to see my family, so it won't be a problem bringing you over to see your friends. Will that worry you, moving away from here?'

Sophie gave it some thought. 'I can still see Stacey?'

He nodded. 'I promise.'

'I suppose I could get a train if you can't drive me over, and she could do the same...but I bet her parents will bring her to see me from time to time. Their relatives live down south.' She nodded thoughtfully. 'I guess it's OK.'

'Good.' His face broke into a grin. 'That's a relief. Now, if you're settled here in front of the TV, Becky and I will retreat to the kitchen.' He handed her the remote control. 'Want a video, magazines, anything?'

Sophie laughed as he piled magazines and the newspaper onto the low table beside the settee. Then, as an afterthought, he tossed her sketch-book and charcoal onto the pile.

'I think you've thought of just about everything,' she said. 'Go away and leave me in peace, will you?'

He didn't need any urging. He took hold of Becky's hand once more and led her from the room. 'We'll have to look for a bigger house,' he said. 'What with Sophie and all the children that might come along after we're married, we'll need a lot more rooms. Then there's the study, and perhaps a playroom—'

'I thought you said you didn't want children,' Becky interrupted.

His expression became serious. 'I think I said I wasn't sure. . .I was caught up in all that Rachel was going through. . .but I can change my mind, can't I? I quite like the idea of having a house full, especially if the girls take after their mother. . .'

Sophie's chuckle followed them as they went into the kitchen, and Matthew shut the door firmly behind them, taking hold of Becky and kissing her soundly until she swayed dizzily in his arms.

'I love you, Becky,' he muttered, his voice roughened. 'Will you marry me? Say yes.'

'Yes,' she said breathlessly. 'Yes. . .' And he kissed her again.

When they surfaced a long time later, she sighed raggedly and told him, 'I don't think I shall be able to stand up much longer, if you're going to go on kissing me that way. My legs feel as though they don't belong to me.'

He pulled out a kitchen chair and sat down in it, taking her with him onto his lap. Then he touched her brow with his fingers, gently trailing them over her heated skin. 'Hmm. . .definitely feverish,' he murmured. 'What I prescribe is a regular dose of Dr Kingston. Before meals, in between meals, and after meals. . .'

'Will that cure me?' she asked softly, her mouth curving in a deliciously expectant smile.

He shook his head. 'I doubt it, somehow,' he said with a grin. 'But it'll make me feel a whole lot better.'

Tesco, Asda, Safeway and other paperback stockists.

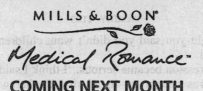

MILLS & BOON

Medical Romance™

COMING NEXT MONTH

MISLEADING SYMPTOMS by Lilian Darcy
Camberton Hospital

How could Dr Megan Stone work with Dr Callum Priestley again, when she couldn't forget the night they had shared two years previously? Callum behaved as if nothing had happened, but now Megan really wanted him to see her as more than a colleague...

OUTLOOK—PROMISING! by Abigail Gordon
Springfield Community Hospital

Dr Rachel Maddox needed a quiet life after her divorce, and her new job and home seemed ideal—until Nicholas Page, eminent neuro-surgeon, began involving her in his life, and trying to organise hers!

HEART SURGEON by Josie Metcalfe
St Augustine's Hospital

Sister Helen Morrisey's sole aim was to be part of surgeon Noah Kincaid's team, because only then did she have a chance of regaining her small son from the Middle East. But she'd forgotten something important, and Noah offered to smooth her path—but what did he gain?

SISTER SUNSHINE by Elisabeth Scott
Kids & Kisses

Widower Dr Adam Brent was sure Sister Julie Maynard wouldn't cope with the job, but she proved him wrong, charming the patients, his two small children—and Adam! But he still wasn't prepared for commitment...

Available from WH Smith, John Menzies, Volume One, Forbuoys, Martins, Woolworths, Tesco, Asda, Safeway and other paperback stockists.

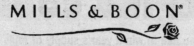

MILLS & BOON®

Marry me
COWBOY

When your lover is a cowboy...

You'll have a stetson on the bedpost
and boots under the bed.

And you'll have a man who's hard-living,
hard-loving and sexy as hell to keep you warm
all night...every night!

Watch it happen in these four delightful new stories
by your favourite authors—
Janet Dailey,
Margaret Way, Susan Fox and Anne McAllister

Available:May 1997   Price: £4.99

Available from WH Smith, John Menzies, Volume One, Forbuoys, Martins, Woolworths,
Tesco, Asda, Safeway and other paperback stockists.

KEEPING COUNT

How would you like to win a year's supply of Mills & Boon®
books? Well you can and they're FREE! Simply complete the
competition below and send it to us by 31st October 1997.
The first five correct entries picked after the closing date will
each win a year's subscription to the Mills & Boon series of
their choice. What could be easier?

$$6 + 3 + \square = 14$$

$$\square + 2 + \square = 15$$

$$\square + 1 + \square = 16$$

$$\square + 6 + \square = 17$$

$$\square + 3 + \square = 18$$

$$\square + 1 + \square = 19$$

$$\square + 5 + \square = 20$$

C7D

PLEASE TURN OVER FOR DETAILS OF HOW TO ENTER ☞

How to enter...

There are six sets of numbers overleaf. When the first empty box has the correct number filled into it, then that set of three numbers will add up to 14. All you have to do, is figure out what the missing number of each of the other five sets are so that the answer to each will be as shown. The first number of each set of three will be the last number of the set before. Good Luck!

When you have filled in all the missing numbers don't forget to fill in your name and address in the space provided and tick the Mills & Boon® series you would like to receive if you are a winner. Then simply pop this page into an envelope (you don't even need a stamp) and post it today. Hurry, competition ends 31st October 1997.

Mills & Boon 'Keeping Count' Competition
FREEPOST, Croydon, Surrey, CR9 3WZ

Eire readers send competition to PO Box 4546, Dublin 24

Please tick the series you would like to receive if you are a winner

Presents™ ❏ Enchanted™ ❏ Temptation® ❏
Medical Romance™ ❏ Historical Romance™ ❏

Are you a Reader Service Subscriber?   Yes ❏   No ❏

Ms/Mrs/Miss/Mr_____

(BLOCK CAPS PLEASE)

Address _____

_____

_____ Postcode_____

(I am over 18 years of age)

One application per household. Competition open to residents of the UK and Ireland only.
You may be mailed with other offers from other reputable companies as a result of this application. If you would prefer not to receive such offers, please tick box.   ❏

C7D